Narratives of Loving Resistance

Two Stories

Studies in Austrian Literature, Culture, and Thought

Translation Series

General Editors:

Jorun B. Johns
Richard H. Lawson

Erich Hackl

Narratives of Loving Resistance
Two Stories

Translated and with an Afterword
by
Edward T. Larkin

Ariadne Press
Riverside, California

Ariadne Press would like to express its appreciation to the
Bundeskanzleramt -- Sektion Kunst, Vienna for assistance in publishing
this book.

.KUNST

Translated from the German
Entwurf einer Liebe auf den ersten Blick and *Geschichte eines Versprechens*
© 1999 and 2004 Diogenes Verlag AG, Zurich, Switzerland

Library of Congress Cataloging-in-Publication Data

Hackl, Erich. 1954 -
　　Narratives of Loving Resistance. Two stories / Erich Hackl ;
translated and with an afterword by Edward T. Larkin.
　　　　p.　cm. -- (Studies in Austrian literature, culture, and thought.
Translation series)
　　ISBN 1-57241-138-4 (pbk.)
　　Contents: Love at first sight: a recollection -- History of a promise.
　　　I. Larkin, Edward T. II. Title. III. Series
PT2668.A2717E5813 2006
833'.914--dc22
　　　　　　　　　　　　　　　　　　　　　　　　　　2005043609

Cover Design
Art Director: George McGinnis

Copyright © 2006
by Ariadne Press
270 Goins Court
Riverside, CA 92507

All rights reserved.
No part of this publication may be reproduced or transmitted
in any form or by any means without formal permission.
Printed in the United States of America.
ISBN 1-57241-138-4
(trade paperback original)

Contents

Love at First Sight: A Recollection 5

History of a Promise 51

Afterword 103
Edward T. Larkin

Acknowledgments

I would like to thank the following for their careful reading of the translation and for their constructive criticisms: Prof. Jacqueline Vansant of the University of Michigan-Dearborn; Prof. David Richman, Prof. Darby Tench Leicht and Prof. Diane Freedman of the University of New Hampshire; Prof. Geoffrey Howes of Bowling Green State University.

Love at First Sight

A Recollection

> To my heart it's all the same
> Whether the bells shoot
> Or the canons ring
>
> Danilo Kis
> "Hochzeitsgäste"

1

In January '37 the Austrian Karl Sequens was hospitalized in the city of Valencia with a bullet wound in his thigh. It is not known for sure where, when, or even how he was wounded. It is a fact that he was brought to the hospital with the other wounded international volunteers; it is also a fact that Herminia Roudière Perpiñá and her sister Emilia responded to a call from the local women's committee to visit these fighters for Spain's freedom and to render their stay in the hospital as short as possible. The women brought fruit and tobacco, and they offered to wash the freedom fighters' clothing, if and when the need arose. They also took letters, written to friends and family members, to the post office, and they bought foreign newspapers for the patients.

When Herminia entered the room where the less seriously wounded lay, the position of one particularly tall patient caused her to smile – Karl measured six feet one inch or even six feet three. Since the hospital beds (like most beds in Spain) were rather short, the young man had stuck his legs through the rails of the footboard and rested his feet on a nearby chair. Perhaps Herminia still had a smile on her face when they looked into each other's eyes for the first time. It was, as their daughter says, love at first sight.

2

Karl's unusual family name can be traced back to the fourteenth-century. Around 1360 the Luxemburg Emperor Charles IV had commanded his German artisans to settle Bohemia. The immigrants who complied demonstrated their obedience by taking the Latin name Sequens (from *sequi* "to follow, succeed"). Karl's ancestors settled in Chotěboř, where for generations they plied their trade as cloth makers and attained a measure of prosperity. But toward the middle of the nineteenth century the family became impoverished as a result of the powerful competition from the British and Dutch manufacturers. Karl's grandfather had to work as a tinsmith in a factory in Brünn. His son, Karl's father, followed in his father's footsteps. He completed a three-year tour in the military with the artillery in Bosnia, moved to Vienna, and then entered the royal and imperial civil service, where he ultimately became a minor civil servant. In 1904 he married Rosa Maria Kolibal, the daughter of a professional colleague in Moravian Tischnowitz. Karl was born the following year, and Rosemarie in 1906. The two siblings grew up in Vienna-Floridsdorf, in a small room in an apartment house for the families of railroad workers (18 Angerer Street); sink and toilet were in the hallway.

3

Herminia's father came from Le Mas d'Azil, a village in the Department of Ariège, about sixty kilometers south of Toulouse. As a young man, he tried his fortune in Valencia, founding a factory that processed animal horn into combs, buttons, and belt buckles. Victor Roudière was competent, and the business flourished. He soon opened a second plant in Barcelona and traveled between the Catalonian metropolis and Valencia. Only when his material existence seemed secured did he ask for the hand of Francisca Perpiñá; her father, however, the owner of an estate in Massanassa, wanted a Catholic son-in-law, and Roudière was a Protestant. So Victor boned up on his catechism, was baptized, and married Francisca with the blessing of his pastor. In 1906 Herminia was born; Luis, who even as a child scorned his baptismal name and always wanted to be called Emilio, arrived in 1908. In February 1911, after the birth of Emilia, her second daughter, Francisca died of childbed fever. Convinced that his children needed a feminine presence, Roudière wanted to marry again. But all unmarried women in the city, who were of his social standing and whom he liked, were terrified of having to replace the mother of three children. His long and arduous search finally ended when he married María Báguena, a young woman from a poor family. Herminia's stepmother could hardly read and write, and it did not take long before the different life experiences and the cultural abyss between husband and wife led to conflicts. These were caused less by the inadequate education of the wife than by the impatience of the husband. They separated after a few years, but when their common son was struck by a severe illness, their concern for him, along with their guilty consciences, persuaded them to give the marriage another try.

Victor Roudière did not fit the image of the unscrupulous entrepreneur who seeks only his own advantage. In spite of the arrogance which he revealed in his second marriage he had a social conscience and was convinced of the need for political reform. He sent his children to a nondenominational school, the *Institución Libre de Enseñanza*, where they were taught to believe in human reason, and he considered each of them, regardless of gender, a serious conversation partner. Herminia owed him not only her excellent command of French but also her drive to acquire knowledge, her willingness to provide help where needed, the ability to stand on her own feet, and the need to understand the outside world as a part of her own world. When she was seventeen, she went to the university to study medicine, but in 1924 her father died. A victim of fraud, Victor Roudière had lost control of the company even before his death; as a result, the children had to break off their studies to earn money for their own survival. The two sons became drivers, and Emilia learned to be a seamstress. Herminia worked as a sales clerk in a record shop and then in a shoe store. When she met Karl Sequens, she was a bookkeeper in a furniture factory. She was thirty years old and still single. Of course, she had had many suitors; several doctors sought her hand, as had a bullfighter, but she had never felt as close to anyone as she did to this stranger.

Her heart was won, says her daughter, by Karl's profound earnestness, which she observed in their first, brief conversation in French. The only people who still remember Karl today confirm this trait. Hans Landauer, who at sixteen went off to fight in the Spanish Civil War, speaks of Karl as a "particularly likable, quiet, and considerate" comrade. A second former volunteer, Alois Peter, calls him "upright, capable, intelligent," and the third, Bruno Furch, recalls Karl as "serious, reflective and also clever." According to him, Karl never clowned around, never acted improperly.

4

It is hard to say how and when we acquire virtues that are not inculcated at an early age. After the collapse of the monarchy Karl's father opted for Austria in 1919; he worked as a company tinsmith for the Austrian Railways. He was a committed Social Democrat. That doubtless colored his son's character, but it did not fully explain it. My view of Karl has much more to do with the volatile social conditions, the years of hunger during the First World War, the proclamation of the Republic, the cultural and social accomplishments of Red Vienna, and the secured future of the young workers. Perhaps he decided to go to Spain on 15 July 1927 when the commander of the Viennese police force had hundreds of demonstrators shot: a violation of trust and law, an insight into the futility of pure hope, a desire to intervene in the course of events.

Three months earlier, on April 4, Karl had begun his military service with the Third Viennese Infantry Regiment; he would serve six long years in the armed services. Out of necessity? – because he saw no future in his learned trade as tinsmith and heating technician. Out of conviction? – because he thought it was precisely the army that needed socialistic elements. Or perhaps of his own volition? – because he liked sports and hoped to pursue his hobbies. The military evaluations from the years 1930 and

1931 indicate that Karl, who had become a marksman in the First Lower Austrian Infantry, did not gain the confidence of his superiors. He was said to be secretive and to lack the necessary degree of commitment and fervor. "Intelligent and very good ability to conceptualize, could perform significantly better." Karl was active in track and field, he was a long-distance swimmer, he was an excellent cartographer, and he was very well trained in the use of light machine guns.

After his discharge from active service, according to his sister Rosemarie, Karl is said to have worked in a factory in Korneuburg that manufactured railroad cars. Then he joined the *Republikanischen Schutzbund*, the Social Democratic defense corps, and in 1934 he took part in the February Rebellion in Floridsdorf. After the rebellion was put down, he fled to Czechoslovakia, where he was taken in by his uncle Roman Sequens, who had become Director of the Post Office in Brünn. From there he went on to Riga. He didn't return to Vienna until the spring of 1936. But one can glean from a report of the Austrian Embassy in Warsaw that Karl Sequens, along with twelve other Austrian members of the *Schutzbund*, was expelled from Lithuania in March 1934: "Sequens was in Riga for approximately two years, as a contact man for the Social Democrats." This assertion is supported by information from the Central Registry in Vienna: Karl Sequens notified the authorities on 6 June 1932 that he was leaving for Riga, and he seems to be back in the sixth district of Vienna on 4 June 1934 at Brauergasse 6 / 5. As of 30 November 1936 he is no longer a registered resident of Vienna. Under the column "Destination" one reads the laconic "departed." His name is included on the list of an illegal cell (November 25) that organized the transportation of volunteers to Spain. And according to a medical report of the International Brigade, Karl arrived in Spain on 26 November 1936.

As he crossed the border, the battle for Madrid was raging. On 6 November the seat of the government of the Republic was quickly moved to Valencia. Franco's troops were finally beaten back on the Casa de Campo and on the university campus. It is possible that Karl was sent to the front after spending a few days in Albacete, the headquarters and training center of the International Brigade. This supposition is supported by the rumor that he was wounded in Campo del Moro, a park between the old royal palace and the western bank of the Manzanares. It is conceivable, however, that he moved with the Thirteenth Brigade to Aragon in the middle of December, and participated in the assault on the city of Teruel, where the Fascists had entrenched themselves. Here or there, shortly after his arrival, he is said to have been hit by the bullet to which he owes his great love.

5

Herminia had once given in to a Gypsy who had absolutely insisted on reading her cards. The woman told her that the señora would be the recipient of the great love of a good gentleman. In response to Herminia's good-natured question, whether her lover was blond, dark, or dappled, the Gypsy replied that she could not determine that, but one thing was certain: the good man wore a uniform. Oh, sighed Herminia, I'll marry a mailman.

She remembered this now in her suddenly impassioned love for Karl, to whom she brought Russian newspapers (she too loved the new Russia which did not

12

abandon Spain), and with whom she spoke about art and literature (for example about Rilke's poems, which he had left with his sister when he departed and which he now wished he had with him, or about the books by the Valencian author Blasco Ibáñez, which he presumably read in German, and she wanted to take him to Albufera, the site of one of Ibáñez' novels, after he recovered). Her Karl, whose shoulder she hardly reached (so she wore shoes with high heels), was not preoccupied with pleasures. In every free minute he wrote or read, or he flipped though his Spanish dictionary (and he confided to her his secret desire to work as a journalist). Karl treated her with respect, never took liberties with her, and she never needed to pretend to be other than who she was. He loved her and not the image of her that he created.

This is how I imagine their love.

And I also learn that Herminia feels transported back to the time she spent with her father, to conversations and debates about what humanity is able to do and what it failed to do. It was, says their daughter, a relationship in which nothing seemed lacking.

6

They were married on 7 February 1937. At most three weeks passed from the time they first saw each other (when Karl was positioned oddly in his bed) to the time their eyes first met, to the time they exchanged rings. The announcement, the official notice of the intended marriage, and the submission of the necessary documents in a certified translation would hardly have been possible, even in peacetime, without help. But Antonio Ferrer, who had married into the family of Herminia's stepmother, knew the local registrar from his childhood, or he was a cousin of the public prosecutor, or he had once done a favor for the mother of a department head in city hall. The bureaucratic process was also accelerated by the uncertainty of what tomorrow would bring and by the gratitude toward a stranger who had come from so far away to risk his life for the Spanish Republic and the Spanish people.

Sí, quiero. Sí, quiero.

There was only time for a single wedding photo. It shows Karl in wide uniform trousers, a light jacket, and cap pulled deeply onto his forehead; he is holding Herminia's hand. They smile shyly, amused, mischievously. Also smiling are the friends, relatives, and passers-by who had joined the celebration, as is customary in Spain. Nothing clearly identifies the occasion: it could just as well have been a family gathering or a company party. The reason for the festivities is only apparent to those who have a keen eye or ear. With a sharp eye they would see the star of the People's Army that the soldier to the left of Herminia wore above his breast pocket instead of the designation of his rank. Their acute hearing could help them detect a few of the fourteen stories that the photo wants to tell, one about each person in attendance.

The little girl, for example, on whose shoulders the soldier's hands rest, is a war orphan. At some point she hopped off a cart carrying refugees or crawled out from under rubble. Presumably she is still alive, a woman of about seventy, a grandmother, widowed. And Antonio Ferrer is still alive, the delicate man with the mustache in the second row all the way to the left. He is said to be quite ill at present; I hear that he has withdrawn from society and that one can no longer speak with him. This is

Antonio, without whom the marriage, as I said, would not have come about so quickly. The photo itself would not have been possible without Emilia (to the right of Karl). For days she searched the town high and low for photographic paper, which she found either in a public office or in a company that was important for the war effort. Friends of friends probably gave it to her. It is also likely that Emilia herself would not have been in the photo if it had not been for the woman next to her. I don't know her name. I only know that twenty-six years before the wedding this woman had nursed Emilia because her own mother had died after giving birth to her. Otherwise I have little more to tell, except that Antonio is standing next to his wife Maruja and that the woman with the glasses and the young man in the light suit are journalists, friends of the Roudière Perpiñá family. It could be that professional interest drew them to the ceremony; the occasion would certainly justify their presence. Although everyone is standing with both feet firmly on the ground (behind them on the left is the Palace of Justice in Valencia, on the right a tree top), the picture has something provisional about it, as if the participants all had come together for just this one moment.

Before I put the photo down, I want to look at the bridal couple again. Karl, Herminia. They knew, says their daughter, that they would have only a short time together.

7

It is difficult to trace Karl's steps through the first year of the war. But Hans Landauer can help with his fabulous memory and the richness of his archive. There are also lists on which Karl's name appears. And there are two accounts by Austrian volunteers which mention him. He also authored four or five articles himself. Thus I know or believe: that after his recovery Karl attended an officers' training school in Pozorrubio. That he subsequently was assigned to the training battalion in Madrigueras as a lieutenant. That in May 1937 he was in Guadalajara where he communicated his knowledge of topography to Austrian comrades who were to be stationed as partisans behind the lines of the Fascists. ("For example, he teaches us," wrote Karl Soldan, "how to travel at night by using a map or compass or by referring to the stars.") That he participated in the battle of Brunete in July as a contact man for the February Twelfth Battalion. That he was wounded in August a second time, either by a sharpshooter or by a grenade fragment, near Quinto, Belchite or Mediana. That he convalesced from his wound in Benicàssim in September. That *Pasaremos*, the newsletter of the Eleventh Brigade, published his article "The Duty of our Stripes" on 25 December 1937. In his commentary Karl appeals to the conscientiousness of all the volunteers: "Our struggle for freedom is hard. It is therefore absolutely essential that everyone give his best for the people. Every fighter can improve, can take on positions of responsibility and leadership, and can achieve distinction. But the people demand that every fighter be ever conscious of his responsibility and that he use all his ability, intelligence, and strength for the people. Each one of us also has the ability to see his errors and to make up for them through his actions."

Karl and Herminia are able to maintain their relationship in spite of all adversity. Karl returns to Valencia as often as possible. Or Herminia visits him at the base in Albacete, or in Valls when he has leave, or in the military hospital at Banicàssim. Or he sends her a note, "am here or there on this or that day," and she finds her way to the remote village, waits for hours on the side of the road before a Soviet officer takes her in his camión, and even allows her to sleep in his tent since she cannot find a room. Just like that, no self-doubt, and on the next day, after a long and often futile search, when she begins to despair, she finds him, finally. In the summer or fall of 1937, Herminia is pregnant.

8

In January '38, on the twenty-fifth, Karl's comrade, Karl Kaspar, was killed. They had taken over an enemy machine gun position near Teruel and had come across a badly wounded officer, whom the fleeing team had left behind in their haste. In spite of the officer's request that they shoot him, they bandaged him as best they could, then left to search for the sharpshooter – who had them in his sights again. After they had gone only a few meters, Kaspar suddenly fell to the ground, hit in the throat by a bullet. Karl bent over him and heard his last words: the request not to let the severely wounded officer die. On the next day when the enemy fire had subsided, Karl and his friend Albin Mayr set out to fulfill Kaspar's final request. They placed the Spaniard on a stretcher and carried him two or three kilometers to the infirmary. As Mayr wrote decades later, the man was not able to explain the care he received. He had always heard horrors about the Reds, and especially about the members of the International Brigade. When they handed him over to the first-aid worker, the officer gave them his address. Visit my family; they will be eternally grateful to you.

Likewise in January '38, on Sunday the twenty-third, Valencia was bombed by German and Italian planes. Fearful of being buried alive, Herminia had never gone to an air raid shelter. This time she again remained at home. When she opened the door to the stairway, she was immediately hit by a blast of air, and she felt something running down her leg: her water had broken. As he took Herminia to her relatives' estate, the driver hit every pothole, hoping to initiate the birth process. And indeed that very evening Herminia gave birth to a healthy girl. In spite of her stepmother's wishes, who believed that the first-born child should be named for one of the parents, Herminia called her child Rosa María, like Karl's mother and his sister.

I don't know why she did not register Rosa María right away. Perhaps because she had to be sutured and spent the first couple of days in bed. It was also probably customary in those days for the father of the child to go to the registry office, and she had promised Karl that she would not take this duty from him. But in the meantime all contact between the two had broken off. For weeks there was no word of Karl, and then within a few days several letters would arrive, letters he had written months before. During the day Herminia would try to ignore the sympathetic looks and the whispers of the neighbors; at night she would cry in her pillow. Until one evening when Karl appeared in the doorway, exhausted, filthy, and hungry. I see him as he takes his little daughter, the child of eight months, into his arms, concerned not to hurt her, how he strokes her soft hair, and feels her tiny fingers. Rosa, Roserl, Rosette. He wishes he could be with Herminia and his child in the city of his own birth; in May they would go to a Ferris wheel in the Prater, in July to the zoo at Schönbrunn, in September to a clearing in the Viennese Woods, in January to the Old Donau Park for ice-skating.

At the town hall he was told that he had unfortunately missed the registration deadline: each birth had to be recorded within five days.

And what do I do now, asked Karl.

A slight bending of the rule, said the official. We will simply push your daughter's date of birth forward a little bit.

To which day?

To today.

Agreed, said Karl.

As the official took the document out of the drawer, he put on a ceremonial face. Then he took the cap off of his fountain pen. Name of child, he wrote, Rosa María Sequens Roudière. Date of birth, 4 March 1938.

9

I know how the story continues. And because I know it, I paint the year '38 in dark colors: battles lost, offensives broken off, positions abandoned. Retreat, advance, retreat. Franco's troops occupy Teruel a second time, throw more divisions at Aragon, and split the Republican position in the mountains. On 25 July the battle at the Ebro begins, on 15 November the people's army yields to the superior force, and in early December Franco attacks Catalonia. Black, deadly black the year 1938. But Karl's reports, which detail the battles that the February Twelfth Battalion fought, are encouraging even if they do not gloss over the reality of the events. That is not only because Karl clearly depicts the effort of the international volunteers against the superior foe; but rather, in spite of all the defeats, he appears to be convinced that the antifascist resistance will become a significant historical force. The reports additionally suggest that he needed to continually reassure himself of the vitality of nature: of the "brilliant spring day" near Mora la Nova, of the "blazing morning sky" by Azaila, or of the "shadows of the twilight" and the "silence of the night" at the banks of the Ebro. The latter he experiences "as redemption . . . as a liberation." Deep blue skies over the village of Torroja, small ship-like clouds above the vineyards, the river, the fresh green of the buds and the young leaves. And the whitewashed houses, the peasants' irrepressible confidence in the international volunteers, the soldiers' embarrassed gestures as they give the women and children tins of condensed milk.

Neither do the two photos taken at the front – shortly before the retreat near Batea, and shortly after the "annexation" of Austria – change the confident tone of his writings. Smiling he stands next to the similarly grinning staff officers of his battalion: none of them know that three of them are on their way to Dachau, that the fourth will perish in the Red Army, the fifth and sixth will parachute unsuccessfully over Germany, the seventh and the eighth will fight with the Yugoslavian partisans after finding their way across the Sahara and the Soviet Union, the ninth will outlive all the others by years, yet finally die a lonesome and bitter death.

In September, the Republican government had withdrawn the volunteers from the front. It hoped that the western democracies would be willing to provide some support. But the governments in London and Paris had already long become indifferent to the fate of the Spanish Republic. In early '39 the massive flight to France began.

10

Rosa María says that her mother had two reasons to flee Spain. First, she was worried that she would be denounced and then arrested after the defeat. Secondly, there was the promise that she and Karl had made: they would never abandon each other.

I want to be where you are.

Karl and Herminia meet for the final time on 2 January 1939 in Gerona. As they parted, they suspected that it would be a farewell for a long time. Once again the international volunteers gathered for a battle; this second deployment was aimed at disrupting the advance of the Fascists, at providing some cover for the fleeing civilians, at postponing the defeat for a few days. The small group of Austrian volunteers, as they were separated from the rest of the troops, soon understood the hopelessness of their undertaking. But the base commander of the International Brigade, a Frenchman by the name of André Marty, threatened to have anyone who defected from the front line shot.

Karl reached the border on 9 February and was interned in the camp at Saint-Cyprien with his compatriots. In Landauer's archive there is a precise, detailed account of their first days on French soil: the view back to Spain, the harsh "Allez, allez!" of the *Garde mobile*, the attempts at extortion by the French legion, the hunger, the lice, the sand storms. "A gray crust of sand immediately covers the bread, plates, suitcases and clothes. Sand fills the pages of opened books before they can be read. At night the wind blasts sand into the eyes and necks of those who try to sleep; you can hear teeth crunching grains of sand when food is eaten." But Karl also mentioned the solidarity of the prisoners, their resistance to the harassment of the camp administration, the mutual help they provided, the announcement of the first anniversary of the occupation of Austria on March 12, then the transfer to Gurs, where the Austrians founded an education center and taught each other foreign languages, mathematics, history and geography. "We have been in the concentration camp for three months now, but our will is not broken, we grow stronger, and our pulse beats ever more powerfully." The nine-page document was smuggled out of the camp, along with an accompanying letter to the editor of the *Deutsche Volkszeitung* in Paris, in which Karl asks for advice and criticism "for your *help* in order to move forward, in order to write *better*."

11

Herminia also landed in Gurs. In January '39 she had fled over the Pyrenees wearing only low-cut shoes. She carried a small suitcase and Karl's military blanket, in which she had wrapped Rosa María. Gurs was a better camp than Saint-Cyprien; at least there were barracks to live in. But when it rained or when snow fell, as it did for days that winter, Herminia sank up to her ankles in the mud. It is conceivable that, restless, she trudged over to the fence that separated the men from the women on one of these muddy days. It is conceivable that Karl approached the entanglement of barbed wire from the other side, that they saw each other one more time. For it is possible, though it cannot be proved, that they were imprisoned in the camp at the same time. Perhaps then Herminia would not have gotten pneumonia, and she would have fought the illness from the very outset. But the way things turned out, she got worse and worse; her fever continued to rise, and the medicine did not help. Herminia only improved when she was encouraged by a nun in the hospital where she was finally admitted: Madame, you must keep going, you have a child! The next night the fever sank, and Herminia was over the worst.

One day the Spanish women and their children were put on a train and sent to Normandy, to Bayeux, where they were housed in a cloister and then in a school. Herminia was the first to be set free. You are French of course, said the official in the administration building as he handed her the identity card. And perhaps Herminia answered: Is it better to be French?

12

In July '40, as the German army pressed farther and farther to the south, the men were evacuated from Gurs and divided up between the camps in Argelès and Le Vernet; some were sent to the Mont Louis fortress. Karl went to Le Vernet, where the prisoners were subjected to particular harassment. The official reason given for Karl's imprisonment was: "Dangerous and extremely active; propaganda against the work requirement." That confirms Alois Peters's supposition that the camp administration considered Karl one of the rabble-rousers among the group of prisoners who had refused the campaign to join the French army.

As early as July, a German commission visited the camp at Le Vernet and called upon the German and Austrian prisoners to return to their respective countries. They were told they had nothing to fear: retraining for a few weeks, then work or military service. Still they resisted. But by the fall, perhaps as a result of a directive from the Communist Party, they were more willing to follow the order.

When the commission showed up in the camp a second time to gather personal information, Karl was asked for his name and his home address. He was interviewed just before his compatriot Bruno Furch.

Sequens, that's a rather old German name! You want to return to the Reich?

And then, after a short pause, yes, yes, Sequens, now comes the consequence. Karl Sequens, as Furch recalls, stood silently ill at ease.

While he was in Le Vernet, Karl was able to establish contact with his sister-in-law in Spain. Since they last met, Emilia had married a legal advisor from Burgos. Like Karl, she too had not heard from Herminia for some time. But she did know that her brothers, who had also fled, were forced into the army as French citizens, and had been taken prisoner by the Germans. The seven letters that Karl wrote to Emilia between September '40 and April '41 show his growing apprehension, even if he was obviously trying to conceal his concern from her. In the very first letter, of 10 September, he informed her of his intention to be repatriated. That was the only possible way to gain his freedom after the rumor that they might be able to go to Mexico had been proved false. He writes that he had nothing to be worried about, only three or four months' stay in a camp where the hygienic conditions were comparable to those in Le Vernet. Then he would be able to rejoin Herminia and Rosa María. "Dearest Emilia, do tell Herminia all of this; tell her to be patient until I find work. Then I will come for her!!"

Karl also wrote to his sister. He did not write directly to Vienna; that would have been dangerous. So he asked Emilia to forward his letters. They no longer exist; Rosemarie probably burned them after she read them. But she did keep Emilia's address in Burgos; later the two sisters-in-law kept each other up to date about Herminia and Karl. Karl's last letter from Le Vernet is dated 4 March 1941: "In a few days I will be gone from here. It is likely that I'll be on my way by the time you read this letter. My joy is indescribable. But I am still troubled about the uncertain fate of my loved ones."

On 5 March Karl was handed over to the German authorities, arrested, and sent to Vienna. Karl was held in the jail on the Roßauerlände so that the Gestapo could interrogate him. His sister was allowed to visit him there once or twice, and he implored her to take care of his wife and daughter. "Do everything in your power to get them to Vienna. And be good to them." I am certain that he knew even then where he would land on 19 January 1942.

13

Rosa María's memories go back as far as the year 1942. Hitler's Germany had long overrun France; it occupied one half of the country and determined what went on in the other half. She recalls a castle ten kilometers outside of Bayeux, on the road to Calais; it served as the headquarters of the German armed forces. She remembers huge vats of cider stored in the castle's cellar, or in the cellar of one of the nearby buildings. She also remembers the administrator's daughter, France, with whom she played. And she remembers the small house next to the castle where the woman who milked the cows lived. This dairywoman, whose name was Madame Marie, repeatedly told the child the tale of the wolf and the seven little goats while Herminia washed and ironed shirts for the German officers. The Germans were very friendly to the child with blue eyes and blond hair, whom everyone knew as Rosette and with whom Herminia spoke only French because no one was supposed to know who they really were.

Sometimes, when Herminia had work to do, Rosette would stay with a woman who kept stuffed animals in her apartment. The animals frightened Rosa María and as a result she did not want to eat her soup. The woman threatened to lock her in the basement, which only caused Rosa María to dislike the soup even more. Or Rosette sat with another woman in the kitchen, next to the stove, when suddenly a pan tipped and spilled boiling water all over her. Rosette screamed and whimpered for days because of the pain. The burns on her upper arm and on her hip did not heal. The doctors believed that only a salve of cod-liver oil would help, but it was very expensive. So Herminia sold the jewelry that she had carried in her small suitcase across the Pyrenees. But Rosette discovered that only much later. That she had a father was also something that she didn't learn until later. She never asked about him, and her mother never spoke of him. "Whenever I saw a man who was kind to me, I called him Papa. But I never had the idea myself that I could have a father. I was rather quiet as a child; I didn't talk about what I had seen or heard. But I also never had the feeling that my mother wanted to hide anything from me. And my mother never showed her concerns. She always acted as if everything was fine."

It wasn't fine: Karl's absence and the uncertainty whether he was still alive; the uncertainty also about

Herminia's siblings and friends and relatives at home; the oppressive poverty, the secret identity, the war, and the fear that the German occupiers would sooner or later become interested in them. When Herminia was not feeling well, she would refrain from writing letters because she did not want to trouble others with her worries. Instead, she preferred to wait until the next day. "Tomorrow it will be better, then I'll write." But during their stay in Bayeux, it did not get better the next day, and so hundreds of letters went unwritten.

At some point Emilia succeeded in finding out Herminia's address. Or Herminia gathered all her courage and wrote to her relatives in Valencia, hoping not to compromise anyone. The relatives in Valencia got in touch with Emilia in Burgos, who wrote to Herminia in Bayeux and to Rosemarie in Vienna. Rosemarie wrote to Karl and to Herminia. And Karl wrote to Herminia, the first of three letters.

14

Dachau, 14 November 1943

My dearest Herminia, it has been three years since I last heard from you. For me this has been a time of pain, hardship and worry, and my patience was almost exhausted when our sisters were finally able to determine your whereabouts. I am so happy that I have found you again. I embrace you and kiss you, my beloved wife, and you too, my daughter, whom I have also not seen in such a long time. I heard from Emilia and Rosemarie that you are healthy, as is our Roserl. What does she look like, our dear child, after so many years? I imagine that she has grown quite a bit. Is she still so fair and blond? And you, my dear wife, how are you? My sister has invited you to Vienna. She wants you to come live with her if you are able, and if you think it is right. I too urge you to do so. Ask the German officials nearby for help and protection so that you'll be able to leave sooner and more easily. Prepare your documents. If you are missing some, write to Emilia for them. My sister will do everything she can to help you. You should write her and tell her what you need. You and Roserl can live with her in her house in Vienna. When there is peace, and when I come home, we'll see each other again. Our future home will be Vienna. Just go, go as fast as you can, and all will be well. We'll live our lives exactly as we had before. I'm glad that the long, terrible period of waiting for news of you has passed and that the uncertainty of your whereabouts is also over. Write to me as soon as you receive this letter. Tell me how things stand, how you and Roserl are doing. If I write to you in German, then I hope that you will be able to have the letter translated. You should also write to me in German. I believe that you know why and that you can put up with such complications. Don't worry about me, I'm fine. Please greet all my loved ones and acquaintances, especially Emilia and her husband as well as their family. Give Roserl a big kiss from me. Hugs and kisses to you in love and in fidelity,

Karl

15

She could have confided in one of the soldiers who were quartered in the castle. (They weren't all Nazis; one had actually asserted that the war would end disastrously for Germany.) The doctor's wife, for whom she did the wash, crocheted blankets and embroidered tablecloths, would certainly have helped her decipher the letter. In addition, she knew the French wife of one of the Germans. (In the picture from Bayeux, Rosette is standing in front of two young women who were friendly with the German soldiers.) But Herminia read the letter in her room, in the house of the Jamais family in Rue Juridiction number 43, without asking others for help. She also wrote the reply without assistance. She had picked up some German in the castle, and the rest she simply figured out with the help of a dictionary. But before she responded to Karl's letter, she told her daughter: Rosette, sit down and listen to me carefully. You have a loving father. The Germans have imprisoned him in a camp, but no one needs to know this. He wants us to go to Vienna where we can live with his sister. Vienna is a wonderful city, you will certainly like it. We can . . .

And so on.

I assume that Rosette listened attentively to her. She was happy that she suddenly had a father; she was after all only in kindergarten, and the other girls had fathers. On the other hand, she kept her enthusiasm in check. She had a hard time imagining how her life would be different with a father, whom she did not know and whom she was not even allowed to visit. Vienna, that sounded attractive, and as long as mother was there, she had no fear of anything or anyone.

But first Aunt Rosemarie had to apply to the Spanish embassy in Vienna to have their birth certificates and Herminia's marriage certificate forwarded. This took several weeks, and then Herminia submitted her application to the German consulate for permission to relocate. And once again considerable time elapsed. Finally, Herminia was summoned to appear at the central office of the Gestapo in Paris to clear up some unanswered questions. Around 10 April they left Bayeux. At the pension in Paris where they were to stay, a Gestapo officer, a certain Swoboda, was waiting for them. He brought

Herminia and her daughter to a hotel that had a revolving door, a chandelier, a double stairway and thick carpets, which deadened any sound. The girl had to wait in the hall as Herminia followed the man up to the second floor.

Her mother was interrogated for twenty days, says Rosa María. For twenty long days she swore that she was never interested in politics.

Why did you get involved with a Bolshevik?

Because I loved him.

Whoever loves a Bolshevik, also loves Bolshevism.

But it was love at first sight.

Something like this.

Finally, they were permitted to travel to Vienna. She sat with a Czech woman and a Polish woman who could only get about on crutches. Just before the train departed, a young man entered the compartment; he repeatedly tried to get a conversation going. The women answered laconically. Often the train stopped between stations either because of an air raid alarm or because a train with soldiers had priority. Every couple of hours they had to show their papers and their tickets. The conductors had hardly shut the door when the young man began to badmouth Hitler, the Nazis, and the Germans. Allez au diable!! Soon they'll get theirs. Herminia rebuked him, but the two other women said nothing, out of fear. In Munich they had a short layover, and the young man left the compartment. The women breathed a sigh of relief, we are finally rid of him. But as the train prepared to depart again, he reappeared: wearing the uniform of an SS officer. He sat down, and looked out the window to the tracks where forced laborers were busy removing rubble from a recent bombing. Look, he said in German, take a look at these animals.

On 5 May 1944, a brilliant spring day, they arrived at the West Station in Vienna. After having endured the hardships of the trip, Herminia was full of expectation. In addition, Karl's second letter, which had arrived in late February or early March, made her more confident. She did not know that he merely invented the table at which he claimed to write to her. He certainly only wrote that, says Rosa María, so that my mother would not worry.

16

Lublin, 13 February 1944
   My dearest Herminia, I received your letter of 28 December on 10 January, but in the meantime I moved so that I was not able to answer you until today. I do hope that you and Roserl are well and that your situation is such that you can hold out a little longer until Rosemarie is able to help you. Because of the move I too haven't heard from Rosemarie, but I imagine that I will receive a letter from her and she will tell me what you decided. If you already submitted your documents to the German Consulate, then hopefully you will be able to go to Vienna soon. Rosemarie has prepared everything for the both of you, and you will feel at home there. When I arrive, we can find our own place to stay. Rosemarie will tell you her thoughts on this. My dear Roserl, my beloved child, how she must have grown. Please send me a picture of you and her. How I will rejoice to be with you again, my loved ones, after so long, even if it is only through a picture. I will put it on my table and your faces will accompany me while I work. Life is indeed sad: for so long I knew nothing of your whereabouts; now I can't take care of our little daughter. How I would like to have a hand in raising her, to teach her to play, and to show her our beautiful Vienna. When she gets there, it will be just the right time for her to go to school. And please tell her a lot about her father; she should know a great deal about him. She should learn

how to do everything she wants; don't let anyone tell her lies. Our child should grow up and live in a world full of work, peace, and happiness. And you, my dearest Herminia, how long has it been since I stroked your hair, since I kissed you tenderly, since I told you of my love for you, that you were always good to me and were a loving wife and good mother to our child in spite of deprivation and hardship. The years apart have been hard, and only in my dreams have I been able to remember you, our life together, and our love. But with all my strength I see the day coming when we will meet again and when our love will blossom anew. In spite of all the misfortune and adversity, I think of you, and I will make our life together, and with Roserl, just as it was. Time has not stood still, and our life will be more beautiful than ever, without hardship, filled with work, peace and happiness. Hugs and kisses to my little daughter. And please give my best to Emilia and her husband, whom I often thank for the help they gave me when I was in France. Love, hugs, and kisses to you, my dear wife, in unwavering love and devotion.

Karl
Please write to me soon!

17

Suppose that Herminia had been allowed to answer him in Spanish or French. Suppose that she did not have to take into consideration his emotional state. Suppose also that her letters were not subject to censorship. Then she most certainly would have written him that Vienna was a great disappointment. It did not have to do with the shabby appearance of the city, with the grim affectation of its citizens, or with the dangers and burdens of the fifth year of the war, but rather with the behavior of his sister Rosemarie; she viewed Herminia as a rival, a competitor for her brother. At that time, Rosemarie owned a women's hat boutique, which was located in the inner city, Hegelgasse 5, behind Varieté Ronacher. After her formal education as a milliner, she continued her training in Munich, Paris, and Berlin, working in the finest hat salons. She remembered these years not only for the entrepreneurial spirit and technical competence that she acquired, but also for the solid grounding in French, the penchant for the sophisticated life, as well as for a New Year's Eve spent with Luis Trenker in the Hotel Vierjahreszeiten. Rosemarie was slender, attractive, and incredibly self-infatuated. Herminia, by contrast, attached no importance to appearances. She valued education, trust, and human kindness. Besides, she had suffered too much deprivation to be concerned about weight problems and beauty tips. That's why her sister-in-law thought her too pudgy and less classy than Karl's former fiancée, a woman from Riga with whom Rosemarie still corresponded. I don't understand my brother, she once said. Juliane dressed much more smartly than you. Or again: Karl, he really deserved a different wife. Perhaps it was this or some other remark that hurt her so deeply, that caused her to cry so bitterly in front of Rosa María, who had never seen her mother cry before and who didn't know how to act. "I just put my hand over her face. At six, I didn't understand anything, not even German. I just sensed that something deeply oppressed her. Something foreign to her character." In contrast, when Rosemarie felt hurt – for example, when Herminia warned her about one of her admirers who had lost her savings at the gambling table – then she punished Herminia with her lengthy silence. "A dreadful silence."

On the first day they met, the aunt had renamed Rosa María, or Rosette. It just can't be, she said in the streetcar, that the child and I have the same name; no one would know who was meant. How about Gloria? They had no objection, or they didn't dare raise an objection. Gloria attended a kindergarten because her aunt was of the opinion that you have to learn German. Herminia learned German too, at the Berlitz Institute located on the Graben. She also took care of the household in the small apartment on Angerer Street, which the elder Sequens had left to his daughter.

One afternoon Herminia picked her daughter up from the kindergarten a little earlier than usual. You know, your grandfather is visiting us now, your father's father. The grandfather – tall like Karl, uncommunicative like Rosemarie – had brought the little girl a bag of sweets: round, colorful war candies made of confectioner's sugar. The following Sunday he invited the two of them to his small allotment garden on the Bisamberg for lunch. Sequens was married to his childhood sweetheart, Katharina, for a long time. His first wife, Karl's mother, had died in 1929. It is too bad that she is dead, Frau Schemitza, a neighbor, had said once to Herminia. If I may say, she was quite different from her husband and her daughter. She would have spoiled you good and proper!

After her grandfather had left, Gloria begged her mother for a piece of the candy: Mama, can't I have a bonbon?

Not now.

Please! Please!

Well, all right, a half.

Herminia reached for the piece, broke it in two – and was shocked: there was a phonograph needle in the piece of candy. She took out a second one, opened it, and again a needle. The same in the third one.

C'est pas possible, she muttered to herself. Your grandfather, he wants to kill us.

With hands shaking, she stuffed the opened candies into the bag, shoved it to the side, and hugged Gloria tightly.

Instead of helping us they want to kill us here.

She took a deep breath.

Go, go play, she said to Gloria.

Perhaps there was some innocuous explanation for the needles. Perhaps they were put into the candies by mistake, or as a prank not intended for anyone in particular, especially not for Herminia and her daughter. But unfortunately they fit the pattern of Rosemarie's hurtful remarks and the combination of arrogance and suspicion that the other relatives expressed toward them. They found it dangerous to be tied by blood to a family whose husband was in a concentration camp and whose wife was a foreigner. In addition, Herminia refused to go to the air-raid shelter in Vienna when there was an alarm. The neighbors reported this to Rosemarie; listen, they said, that simply cannot be tolerated. And the sister-in-law, Rosemarie, reached a decision: Herminia and her daughter must leave; they will go to the countryside where there was no bombing. Rosemarie had good relations with some influential people; she was herself a member of the Nazi Party, as her niece was to find out later (the hat shop, arianized), and it didn't take long before she said: on 6 July you will be evacuated. To Bavaria, the Oberpfalz.

To Bavaria? asked the elder Sequens. Why are you sending the two of them so far away? Karl will never find them when he is freed.

What are you saying, said Rosemarie, we have their address.

18

In Klardorf-Zielheim, in the district of Burglengenfeld, they were given a room by some farmers. Bare, cracked walls, a wooden floor, a bed. No chair, no armoire, no hot plate. Even the mayor found that a little strange. What's going on here? Why isn't there any furniture? The wife of the farmer, impertinent or in utter conviction: for a French woman it's certainly good enough. But the mayor felt that the honor of his office was aggrieved, and so, at his behest, the farmers had to bring two chairs, an armoire, and a round table into the room. A nightstand was found, and Herminia placed a picture on it, Karl's portrait from the year 1931. And now, said the mayor, they get something to eat. Why, we don't have much ourselves? Finally, ill tempered, they put four fried eggs in front of Herminia and her daughter, and then crossed their arms as they leaned back and watched every bite that the two took, from fork to mouth. There I noticed it again, the division between us and the others, said Rosa María. It wasn't any better at school. Stupid French bumpkin.

Herminia wouldn't let them get her down. The main task was to work. Somewhere she found a sewing machine with which she shortened pants, mended shirts, and reversed jackets. Sometimes she worked in the field, and the women gave her sweet yeast-dumplings filled with fruit, a half-loaf of bread, and occasionally some dried meat in return. The war was drawing to a close; that could be seen from the increasing number of refugees coming from the East: these were women, children and old people who refused to understand their own misfortune through that of others. Herminia sat hunched over her sewing machine for them too.

Toward the end of January or in the early part of February 1945 Herminia received Karl's third letter, postmarked at the office of censorship of the concentration camp Auschwitz III. Just a few simple lines, which reassured her and encouraged her as she held the letter in her hands. The Red Army had liberated Auschwitz. But she did not know that, unless the French prisoner of war who was staying in the inn across from her had secretly heard it on the radio or had picked it up some other way and told her. By and large, he was the only person in Zielheim with whom Herminia could have a conversation, except for Gloria. I assume that Herminia talked to him about Karl; as she tried to hide her fears, he probably detected them. All will be well. You will see.

One day, perhaps it was 16 February, Karl's photo mysteriously fell from the nightstand. Herminia was frightened. As she cleaned up the shards, she blurted out to Gloria, something has happened to your father. Another day, in March or early April, Herminia delivered a patched skirt or a coat with a new lining to the inn. Where is the French gentleman, she asked. Where would he be, said the wife of the innkeeper, in the barn where he belongs. Herminia pushed the barn door open with her foot and took a few steps to where he was sitting on the milking stool. Bonjour Monsieur, she said cordially. Comment allez-vous? He jumped up quickly. He almost knocked over the milk bucket and screamed: What are you doing here? What's the big idea? Get out of here! Perplexed, Herminia mumbled an apology, turned to leave, and stopped out of terror. In the corner of the barn, a shaved, hollow-cheeked skull poked through the cut straw.

I'm sorry, said the Frenchman, I wanted to spare you this sight. The man in the corner has typhoid fever; he escaped from the concentration camp with four of his comrades. He explained that they had made their way as far as Zielheim and that he hid them in the barn for two nights. Help me, he said, bring them something to eat. Herminia ran across the street to her room and cooked some oatmeal gruel, which she poured into a milk can. This took her some time. She refused to connect the haggard face of the refugee with Karl. Until then, she had imagined that the conditions in the German concentration camps were like those of Gurs. Karl's letters had reinforced this belief.

The closer the end of the war appeared, the more she told her daughter of her own childhood, of the uncles and aunts in Valencia, and of the teachers in the school. Of the excursions that she took with her siblings every Sunday, and of one of her admirers, a doctor, who, once on a date with her, sat on a freshly painted park bench and then jumped up angrily when he realized his mistake. Insulted by Herminia's ringing laugher, he turned away from her. She liked to talk about this episode a lot. She spoke little about the notion of love at first sight and about the man whom she had loved at first sight. She wanted Gloria to grow up without this burden, a normal child, only without a father, like many of the war children. That's why, according to her daughter, Herminia put up with so much.

Then came the spring of '45. In Schwandorf, the nearest larger town, several civilians died because an SS man or an army officer didn't want to surrender the little city to the Americans without a fight. Hardly had the war ended when Herminia began her search. She figured she could get information about Karl's whereabouts from the Red Cross or at the Allied information centers in Nuremberg or in Munich. But no one was able to help her, or wanted to. Back to Zielheim, she waited, hoped, and worried. She wrote to Rosemarie: did Karl perhaps . . . , but she didn't know whether her sister-in-law ever received the letter. Then in the late fall a teacher from the neighboring village of Steinberg, Fräulein Berger, looked her up. Berger was an Austrian, from Klosterneuburg. Right at the end of the war she had made her way to Vienna, where she met with Herminia's sister-in-law. She asked me to give you this letter. In it was a note from Rosemarie: "I received this last letter from our dear Karl on 8 January 1945. I heard from comrades who were with him in Auschwitz that they and many others were taken to Sangerhausen in Thuringia (Camp Dora), postal address Neuhausen, in mid-January. The poor souls were transported in open cars in the terrible cold. They traveled for eleven days – without food and without drink. They ate snow. Many had frostbite, including our poor Karl. Many were weak and took ill, our poor Karl as well. There was typhoid fever in the camp at Sangerhausen. Karl is said to have become ill in February. I hope he comes through it. I pray to our dear God and to my dear mother that they release him healthy and that he comes home to us."

19

8 Jan. 1945
My dearest wife, my dearest Gloria. I am terribly happy to have finally received a letter from you. I know that you think of me and that, like me, you too are longing for a reunion. That Gloria is lovely, has grown up, and learns and plays hard is the most wonderful thing there is for us. I am healthy and am always thinking about how happy we will all be in our home some day. Gloria, my dear child, learn as much as you can, but also be happy and play joyfully. Here

are many kisses for you! And here are hugs and kisses for you too, my one and only love. Karl.

20

Still she hoped for a belated return. Who knows, said the neighbors, perhaps the Russians have taken him. They said that with the same firm conviction with which they blamed others for everything that had happened to them. They said it so often that Herminia gradually came to accept this as a possibility. Stalin and his kind, didn't they persecute their own people even in Spain?

But one day, weeks after Fräulein Berger had stopped by, a stranger appeared in Zielheim, Egon Steiner from Vienna; he had fought in the Spanish resistance. He said that he and Karl had promised each other to carry out the final labor of love. That's why he was here. He was present when the prisoners were taken from Auschwitz to Dora Mittelbau in the open cars. He was there when they tried to still the hellish thirst with snow, when Karl lay feverish on the straw, when the SS man raised his pistol and took aim at Karl. About the thin line of blood from Karl's mouth he said nothing. He said (and felt embarrassed for saying it) that his companion's final thought was of her and the child.

Herminia nodded, thanked him, cried, and wanted both to send him away and to keep him there.

When her daughter came home from school, she said: Gloria, your father is dead.

And Gloria thought, now I have to be very strong.

Yes, Mama, that is very sad.

Since I didn't know my father, she says, it didn't hurt very much.

21

Of course, Herminia could have gone with her daughter to France, to Lyon for example, where her brother Emilio had settled as a barber. Or to Spain, to her sister Emilia, who begged her in every letter: Come, stay with us! (And who, a few years later, would take in Victor, on whom the horrors of the Nazi dictatorship had taken their toll.) Or to Vienna, where Rosemarie would have suddenly welcomed her. In her very first letter the sister-in-law had invited her to come and stay with her; she had already rented an apartment with two rooms "one for you two and one for me," after the house on Angerer Street had been destroyed in an air raid.

Vienna, that was Karl's dream and Herminia's love. But she did not want to come empty-handed. She wanted neither to have the city given to her nor to purchase it with Rosemarie's guilty conscience. (She didn't know that Karl's sister, "the only one who had consistently made the greatest sacrifices for her brother," had meat, potatoes, a half kilo of sugar sent to her from the Concentration Camp Association). So they stayed in Bavaria. The widow's pension amounted to twenty-four marks, and the orphan's pension was twelve marks. The rent alone cost twenty marks per month. At first, she managed to support herself and Gloria as a seamstress. But two or three years after the end of the war she crocheted the farmer's daughter a pair of white gloves for the firemen's ball. The gloves caused quite a stir among the girls, where did you get them, tell me; and a few weeks later she received a notice from the district seat that a trade license is required for any remunerative activity. She is hereby summoned to present her craftsman's diploma immediately. She had no diploma and so was forced to look for a different kind of work.

At around the same time, Rosemarie repeated her invitation to come to Vienna. "The People's Association wrote me and asked me to inform you that you will get a monthly pension of 150 Schillings and that Gloria will receive 40 Schillings, in total 190 Schillings. Why don't you come and take it? I am holding your apartment and paying the rent on it; it is completely renovated, with gas cooking, everything is separate, and the windows are recessed with glass. You would live in the city again as you had before. Don't you ever feel like going to the theater or seeing a French movie in the original?

Yes, Herminia did have desires; she longed for Karl, to whom she would have been closer in Vienna. But she also had her pride; she wanted to establish her life there, at the side of the man who was still present to her even in his absence, by her own efforts. One possibility was to deliver newspapers. Herminia and Gloria started out with seven subscriptions, but ended up delivering the *Mittelbayerische Zeitung* to five villages. At some point, she began to write about citizen initiatives, farmers' tales, and carnival parades. And the editors included her articles in the paper. In February 1957 she learned that the orthopedic clinic in Schwandorf was looking for a laundress. Herminia applied, and got the position. Since she was familiar with Greek and Latin terms, which she had learned during her medical studies, she was asked to attend to the patients at night after the operations. One of the doctors liked to talk with her. You are certainly overqualified for your job, he said. You should take a course to become a nurse's aide! And she took the course. She was sixty years old and still dreamed of Vienna.

22

Gloria and the question of being different.

She asked her first question at eight or nine, shortly after the war, when the community let them have a tiny piece of land for their own use. Herminia wanted to plant a few potatoes, tomatoes, and cucumbers, but first they had to clear out the weeds, and for that they needed a hoe. Go run to the farmer and ask him for one. The farmer's daughter looked at her sympathetically: you don't even have a hoe, you're that poor. In bed that evening Gloria asked her mother: Mama, why are we so poor? Herminia: It doesn't matter if you are poor or rich. It matters how you conduct yourself in life. Rich, poor, that is not the question. (Or unfortunately it is, she thought, as she ran her finger across Gloria's cheek, nose and forehead.)

The second question wasn't a question at all. When they delivered the newspapers, Rosa María and her mother had to get up at three in the morning. They picked up the bundles at the train station in Schwandorf, where the early train, which came from the printing plant in Weiden, had dropped them off. Rosa María loaded a pile of newspapers onto her bicycle and set out for the surrounding villages. In school she was tired and unhappy. She was afraid to be called on and give the wrong answer. She was afraid to be ridiculed. She was afraid to be made fun of because of her height – she had grown quickly and towered over the other school children. She was afraid that someone would discover the printer's ink on her palms and fingers. So, since she was not permitted to keep her hands under the desk, she closed them into fists and held them tightly against her upper arms. One morning this caught the eye of her teacher. Herr Schramm, whose hatred of the French had not been cured by his stay in a prisoner of war camp, was not a fully trained teacher. Sequens, he said, show us your hands. She obeyed. The other children strained their necks and laughed. You see, children, said Schramm, this is how dirty the French are. They don't even wash their hands.

The third question she asked more than once, and Herminia answered her more than once. Mama, why do I have to study so much? Why are you so strict with me? Because I am not only your mother; I also have to replace your father. Or: because I don't want you to embarrass me in front of your father. What if he suddenly appears one day at the door. Then you had better be able to show him that you have made something of yourself. A graduate of a nursing program, for example, but this is something which Gloria did not feel herself capable of achieving since her written German was weak – Herminia only spoke French with her. But then she remembered a saying that her mother used to repeat, one which always cheered them up. If we survived the war, we will survive anything, and at eighteen she registered for the nursing program in Hof/Saale. She spent the Christmas holidays at home with her mother. Let Gloria go dancing sometimes, said the farmer's wife, you can't keep her locked up forever. Herminia: the woman is right. Just go out, have some fun, but don't forget who you are.

The fourth question – why she should not forget who she is – was not asked, at first. In the newspapers or in the movies she saw pictures of emaciated figures in striped uniforms. Her father, one of them. There it was again, that oppressive feeling that she had felt as a child. And she knew that she would never be like the others. I will always have to contend with this burden. If someone stood up for her, from the very beginning Gloria would not put up with any misunderstanding between them: my father died in a concentration camp. In Bavaria at that time, she felt she could count on whoever was able to accept her past. Or perhaps not, as the example of her first marriage shows. The young man did not take exception to her high standard; on the contrary, he had passionately courted and admired her. Perhaps she should have been tipped off by the dumb talk of German soil and by the family's collection of medals and ribbons. On the other hand, one marries an individual, not his whole family. But the man was too brusque in his tone and hurtful in his dealings with people; he seemed to enjoy belittling her. She put up with it for six long years. One day he snarled: your father must have been up to something, otherwise they would not have put him away in the concentration camp. Then she left him.

The fifth question, about her citizenship, was resolved in the mid-fifties. Neither she nor Herminia had valid papers at that time. When Gloria took her first job in the hospital in Landshut, she overheard an employee in the personnel department say, what, no identification? She'll no doubt be good for nothing. It was a lengthy and complicated process, but finally the passports were issued – Austrian passports, Herminia attached great importance to that.

The last question – what her real name actually was – was answered on her twenty-fifth birthday, when she went up to Herminia and demanded back her first name. Mama, don't ever call me Gloria again. Call me what you used to: Rosa María.

23

In the fall of 1959, mother and daughter decided, without a moment's thought, to take a second trip to Vienna. Earlier in the year, in February, they had also visited their relatives in Spain. Rosa María was very eager to learn more about her father and his family, but Aunt Rosemarie in Vienna hardly told her anything. She continued to maintain her "dreadful silence" about her own and Karl's childhood, nothing about their parents or their grandparents, nothing about her final meeting with Karl in the police jail on the Roßauergelände, except for one sentence: "Your father gave me the charge to be good to your mother." There was a wall between us, says Rosa María. Perhaps it would have been possible to break it down. But how, and at whose expense? In Spain everything had been different: the relatives in Burgos and Valencia, Seville and Benidorm had received them with open arms and countless expressions of their affection. All-night conversations among the siblings, excursions, invitations, and recollections: do you still remember how . . . And then when . . . Rosa María returned to Bavaria firmly believing Spain was the better place to live.

Herminia was also disappointed that she found no one in Vienna who knew Karl when he was younger. "Personne n'est ici, personne n'est ici." Financial compensation was never granted to her or to her daughter. They even hired a lawyer to help them with their claim. He demanded fifty marks a week, a lot of money in the late fifties. Their whole income was his petty cash. But the German officials rejected their claim, "since someone who fought for the Reds in Spain, who for security reasons was interned in a concentration camp, cannot be proved to have been an opponent of National Socialism."

The German Democratic Republic would have considered his opposition proven. Mother and daughter were even invited to settle there. They would have been given an apartment, a job, and Rosa María could have studied at the university; after all, they were family members of a murdered communist. They refused, Herminia out of principle because she didn't want to accept something as a gift, and perhaps because she feared she might lose sight of her final goal, Vienna. Rosa María out of defiance. My father, she thought, sacrificed himself for the party and for his convictions. And what was the result? Where were all of his comrades? They could have helped, could have stood together, like those where she lived, in the village where the members of the CSU or the Social Democrats stood together. For this reason she never wanted to become a member of a party, just like her mother, who said: I won't have anyone dictate to me what I am supposed to do. When I do something, I want to do it of my own accord, not because it is the order of a party official. Her choice of career was also a result of Karl's fate. As a nurse, we can be there for everyone.

So, no compensation. No news about Karl. It was Rosa María who decades later was the first to come across Hans Hertl and Josef Gansch, the Austrian freedom fighters who served in Spain and remembered Karl. A serious, very serious man, this Karl Sequens. Sometimes a bit didactic. And: you know, he was a man of unimpeachable character, but you could somehow tell that he was from the wealthy Bohemian cloth families. Always so fine and reserved. Another former volunteer, the doctor Josef Schneeweiß, claimed in a phone conversation that he saw Karl die. Karl's lungs got infected in the camp and he died in the barracks. A horrible death. I saw it with my own eyes. Rosa María was devastated. It would have been better if I had not called him at all. But Schneeweiß must have confused Karl with someone else; he can't have been with Karl when he died, since he, Schneeweiß, was imprisoned in Dachau until it was liberated, like Bruno Furch, who also believed that Karl Sequens perished there. I knew, he says, that Sequens had something wrong with his lungs. But Karl was certainly murdered somewhere else, on the way from Auschwitz to Dora Mittelbau, as the report by Egon Steiner suggests. Or he survived the transport and then died later: according to the International Missing Persons Service in Arolsen, Karl Sequens entered the infirmary at Dora Mittelbau on 29 January 1945. He is said to have passed away there at five in the morning on 16 February. Dora Mittelbau, near Nordhausen in the Harz Mountains, an auxiliary camp of Buchenwald.

In the cemetery at Klardorf there is a mass grave for the concentration camp prisoners who were murdered during the death marches shortly before the end of the war. Herminia looked after the grave while she was alive, planting ice ferns, decorating a small Christmas tree, and lighting grave candles. In memory of Karl, so that he knows that we are thinking of him. She never thought of marrying again. She was, as Rosa María says, faithful to my father until her death. This is why I have such profound respect for her.

24

Herminia had always planned to settle in Vienna with her daughter. When her sister-in-law died of a heart attack in

April 1972, she decided that the time had come. In the name of her daughter she put in a claim for Rosemarie's communal apartment. For the first time she was able to take advantage of Karl's engagement for a free Austria. The proceedings dragged on for months. Only in the fall did Rosa María receive a notice that she was to appear in Vienna to sign a contract, and to do so immediately. But Herminia was in the clinic in Schwandorf; she had jaundice and was running a fever, puzzling symptoms of a disease that had been brought about by an incorrectly administered anti-inflammatory. Rosa María did not want to leave her mother alone.

I'll do without the apartment; I'll stay with you.

Out of the question. You will travel to Vienna.

Rosa María gave in, traveled to Vienna, signed the rental agreement, ran to the registration office, and got to know the boorish charm of Austrian bureaucracy. She called the hospital three times a day. No need to worry, she was informed, everything is fine. Then suddenly: her kidneys have failed, she is no longer responsive. When Rosa María arrived on the very next train, late in the night of 28 November, her mother was already dying. At her bed sat a nun who had been active in an African mission and who prayed for Herminia's salvation in three languages. Rosa María recalls: I again realized that my mother was a true cosmopolitan. As one lives, so one dies.

Herminia Sequens was buried in the cemetery at Schwandorf. The parish priest, I assume, praised her Christian conviction and brotherly love. In the name of the clinic, the administrator thanked the deceased for her long years of service to the German public health system. I hear words like self-sacrificing, selfless, reliable. (That he wanted to fire her because of her illness went unsaid.) I also hear Rosa María speak, only one sentence: Mama, I promise you, one day I will write down your story.

25

Rosa María's first thought was to give up the communal apartment in Vienna. (That's impossible, hollered the city official into the phone; first you make us go to all this trouble for you and now you don't want to take the apartment!) To go to Aunt Emilia in Spain who was fond of her and who would gladly have taken her in. Or to stay in Schwandorf, in a more settled environment. She did have a good job, a nice apartment. But then her mother's final words occurred to her. We will not give up your aunt's apartment. You will travel to Vienna! Perhaps she recalled Karl's last letter from Dachau. "Our future home will be Vienna." So she settled in Vienna, her father's city, uncertain whether she would like it in the long run. She took a position in the surgery department in the General Hospital. I suspect she was capable, reliable, serious, like her parents. Perhaps she was also a little lonely. It's possible. It is sad to explore a city over which the shadows of your parents hang. Occasionally, she would see patients in her ward who would be connected to Spain by some invisible thread, like herself. One was a Spanish teacher, who told her of his love for the country, for its people, for its culture. Once again a love story that begins at the foot of a hospital bed, even if not love at first sight, for they reportedly got together only rather slowly, she and Manfred, who was sensitive, loved people and had a thirst for knowledge. Who doesn't put others down, belittle them, or shame them. Who believes he has to be there for all his students. Who, in dealing with others, is moved neither by their arrogance nor by their wealth, but only by the "nobility of their soul." Through him, says Rosa María, she has accepted Vienna as her home. But she would also feel at home in Bavaria or in France. And especially in Valencia: when the pilot banks the plane during an approach to Valencia so that the city appears through the window, the city in which everything began, "then all my heart grows warm." So joyful, so painful.

26

When long ago Rosa María's teacher, the not fully certified Herr Schramm, had preached hatred of her daughter, Herminia took Rosa María by the hand and ran to the school to complain to the principal Isidor Lang. Bit by bit, Herminia divulged the story of her life to this man. Saying nothing for a moment or so after Herminia had finished, the principal then remarked: this love has cost you dearly. And looking at Rosa María, Herminia replied: But it was worth it.

History of a Promise

He had had to make the promise; in this respect he feels no guilt. The woman was carrying the potatoes in the wire basket, stumbled over the hoe, tried not to drop the basket, fell –

She is slender, has long light-colored hair, wears a white blouse, and blue linen pants with a braided leather belt. No glasses. She is sixty, but looks fifteen years younger.

Her question, as always: shall I drive you? He knows that she worries about him. Whenever he meets his friends or has an appointment with a tenant, in a café or in an office, she sits down at the next table and leafs through magazines. Or she waits downstairs in the car.

He never considered telling her. His wife agreed. Never. Simply wrong. Once his wife said, but wouldn't it be better . . . He didn't even let her finish the sentence. No. *End of discussion.*

She most enjoys novels of fate, but she also likes films filled with love, passion, and renunciation. The theme is always the same: a yearning to die for sheer joy.

Sometimes when he sits in the tiny garden behind the house, on the bench next to the grill, he recalls his past. When he compares it to what he has made of himself, his life seems like a dream.

For, what would he have become if the great tragedy had not occurred? A mechanic perhaps, or a criminal.

She studied economics and then worked for years at the phone company. She was later employed in a ministry. Five years ago she was forced into early retirement, but at least she received a decent severance package. For a while she delivered cakes that he had baked at home. The demand for typical Austrian pastries was considerable, but the expense got out of hand, and at some point she lost the desire to continue. What's more, the small pastry shops are gradually closing down; the Chileans think that they can save time and money if they take their coffee on the run.

He still likes to cook and does so quite well: apple strudel, Linzer cake, goulash, schnitzel, stuffed peppers, ham and noodle casserole, and cabbage and noodle casserole.

They share the same house, but he doesn't interfere in her life. She goes out three times a week. She spends one night with her friend, an attorney. But she no longer has any desire to marry.

Until recently she had her own car. Now she takes his. He doesn't want her to ask to use his car. She does so anyway.

He never heard her utter a mean word.

He never concealed anything from her, except for that one particular thing.

He might be called Wilhelm Gubi. Willi. And she Elena,

Hélène, Leni. That would simplify matters. Their real names shall remain a secret.

Not for a moment did Willi consider remarrying.

Elena is also widowed. Her husband passed away some time ago – a fellow student, who even during his studies was often ill. Later they worked in the same department. His father suffered from depression and threw himself out a window one day. Her parents knew that. But when she first brought him home, they kept their concerns to themselves. Only you can know that. We won't stop you, and we won't encourage you either. However you decide, you can always count on us.

Willi was deeply involved with his work when her husband was failing. He had just taken over a large laundry business, with more than fifty employees, in a city where he couldn't trust anyone. He was faced with a choice: to manage the growth of the business or to give up everything in order to be there in her hour of need. It wasn't a difficult decision for him.

Money comes, money goes. Willi's motto. It served him pretty well.

Elena has a wardrobe filled with hats. She's eccentric that way. Buying hats, why not.

Her late husband had received an attractive offer from the US, one that he did not want to turn down. So he worked for a year at a consulting firm in Florida. Elena did not accompany him; she stayed in Santiago with her mother and with him.

As a child she was absolutely convinced that she was the daughter of a prince.

The word "never," the word "always," the word "dreadful": At that time, conditions were terrible in Austria, in Vienna, and in Leopoldstadt. He was always hungry; his belly was never quite full. And he was left on his own. His father, originally a tailor before he worked in the leather industry, was usually unemployed. He was a Communist or at least a sympathizer; he lost the little money he had gambling in the pub. On occasion, his mother was allowed to help out as a cook, for a scrap. Neither one of them had the energy to care for Willi.

Elena never had a strong desire to travel to France. But she and her brother were keen to go to Vienna. Willi didn't have time for that. At first, there was no time at all; then, the trip would have been possible, but there was always some reason to put it off, and now he has lost a lot of his money in the stock market. But sure, he'd like to visit Vienna; he wants to see where he grew up. His old turf included three or four streets – Große Mohrengasse, Schmelzgasse, Zirkusgasse, Ferdinandstraße. He'd also like to visit the school at Czernin Square, his teacher, Mr. Portemonnaie, and the hospital of the Brothers of Mercy.

The apartment in the Große Mohrengasse was a dark, narrow flat with two beds and a dresser. His parents slept in the first bed, and his sister, eight years older, slept in the second. Willi slept on the trunk next to the door. Until one day when he simply took off to a remote lot in the

Zirkusgasse; it was inhabited by old, scrapped trucks. From there he undertook his forays to still his hunger.

Frau Keller of the local grocery store regularly gave him a slice of bread and two pieces of Quargel, an Austrian round cheese. Anticipating a reward, Willi carried her customers' baskets home. The Brothers of Mercy usually had something left over for him. Once, he got some goulash soup at Eminger's, a tavern at the Prater. On Saturdays, Sauer, the butcher on the Graben, gave away the sausage that he hadn't sold. The line ran from the door of his shop across the Kohlmarkt. From the pieces of meat that he could lay his hands on, his mother made a ham and noodle casserole at home. In the Czernin School each child got a small bottle of milk at the ten o'clock recess, except Willi, because his parents couldn't afford the milk. One day the teacher, Mr. Portemonnaie, noticed this. He took the other children aside and urged them to give some of their milk to their classmate. At that instant, Willi could see how wretched his life was. It was so unbearable that he stayed away, forever.

His wife always told her children: If your father claims that it's going to rain upside down, from the ground to the sky, it does so.

At five, he began to steal. His father had finally found a job, as a miner, and they moved to Pitten, located on the Aspang Rail Line. Pitten is a small village with a castle and a church, farmers and apprentice miners. When there were disturbances in the mine among the workers, his father went on strike; he was fired and disappeared for several years, hoping to earn money elsewhere. Mother sat there with her two children, in a hovel at the edge of town, next to a streamlet. She didn't know how she would survive. But she did own a pair of scissors with which she wanted to slit her wrists. Willi snuck up to a farm, found the smokehouse, then the pantry, which contained bread, sugar and lard; he threw it all onto a cart und brought it home undetected. The thefts increased in frequency, and the neighbors became suspicious. On Krampus Day, a celebration of St. Nikolaus's villainous counterpart, someone wanted to get even; Willi put a sharp knife in his belly. The blade was of stainless steel, the handle a rabbit's paw. The police hurried to the scene and wanted to lock Willi up, but he hid on a baker's cart, in the back, among the warm loaves of bread.

On the first of May, Willi's siblings wore starched shirts with red kerchiefs and marched to the City Hall Square. Up front the horns, with schalms or flutes. The army shot at them once, from up on the Reichsbrücke. There was gunfire in the Goethehof. He was nine at the time.

Pepi Nowotny was somewhat younger than Willi; he too had a sister and his father, a Communist, worked for the railroad. When Hitler first occupied Austria, they sat around the kitchen table in Pepi's house and cried, out of anger and because no one had come to their aid. As the steps of the marching soldiers resounded from Erdberger Straße, they heard a droning sound, which grew louder and louder, higher in pitch, deafening. They jumped up, ran to the window, kicked open the shutters, and leaned out. Across the small bright quadrangle of sky above the courtyard thundered a squadron of planes. Joyously they danced around the table. Russian bombers, Soviet flyers will free us from the Nazis.

At fourteen, his sister had found a job selling umbrellas. Five or seven years later she married Paul Blum, a cobbler from Alsergrund. Somehow Willi was able to recover the wedding picture. It now lies in a drawer.

Sometimes Elena picks it up. She thinks that she looks very much like her aunt.

She also thinks that she looks like her own brother. The high cheekbones and the bold turn of the eyebrows.

His brother was some ten years older. He was a talented draftsman, whom his aunt took in. There he did not have to go hungry, and he returned to Vienna as a trained lithographer. When the Germans marched in, he was fulfilling his military service. Two days after the invasion, he fled to Switzerland.

Willi still speaks with a genuine Viennese dialect, and Elena answers him in Spanish. She spoke French with her mother.

Around eight o'clock on April 9, 1938, the evening before the plebiscite to determine if Austria was to be annexed into the German Reich, Hitler was traveling in an open car along the Praterstraße. The street was heavily lined with marshals, police, and jubilant crowds. At Nestroy Square, or perhaps a little further down the street, at the corner of Rotensterngasse, someone threw a red flag onto the car. For a fraction of a second Willi observed it float down over the heads of those in the crowd in front of him. They then had to lie on the ground for hours, arms outstretched, face on the pavement, while SA men and Gestapo officials fluttered about excitedly.

He did not know that he was a Jew; now he knows it, but he doesn't feel different.

One day during the summer he was walking with Pepi Nowotny along the Ring. A man in a brown coat approached them; he jostled Pepi from the sidewalk and hissed at Willi: Shame on you. A German boy like you, in the company of a Jewish troublemaker. Pepi had dark hair, a narrow face, full lips. Of course he wasn't Jewish.

Sometimes he looks at Elena and tries to recall the face and figure of her mother. A similarity, or a difference. He is unable to say. He sees nothing, he can't see anything, because for a long time he has not wanted to see. He doesn't deny it: he has done everything in his power to erase the woman from his memory.

The day after the pogrom Willi's father was playing cards in the tavern on Ferdinandstraße. Willi sat close to the table hoping that the winner would slide him some change. Suddenly SA troops stormed into the pub and dragged them off: him, his father, and a few others. They were brought to the office of the police superintendent at the corner. The next morning they were transferred to the barracks. All men except for another boy of his age. Anyone who spoke was whacked with the night stick. That wasn't really so bad, he was used to beatings. Then they were forced to stare into the blinding light of the ceiling lamp. Silly, stupid things. A few days later, his father was called out, along with five or six others. There was no time for a final good-bye. Afterwards he heard that they had been hanged. Over the years Willi has found out the truth: on 1 December 1940 his father Georg died in Gurs, the transit camp near the Pyrenees in France. How did he get there? The question is of little interest to Willi. No one can make his father come back to life.

Nor does the other question bother him: exactly when and where they locked his father up in one of the transports. Had weeks or months gone by? Was he held in the barracks the whole time? Was his mother allowed to visit him?

A nun with a harelip. The crib with the iron bars. The torture of having to sit for hours on the potty. Elena doesn't remember it, but she knows it. He told her about it. His wife had also told her. There is only one thing that she doesn't know. Her life is logical and clear.

Willi was thirteen when he got on the transport. He was fourteen when he was transferred from Buchenwald to Dachau. Sixteen and seventeen at Birkenau, seventeen-and-a-half in Auschwitz, eighteen in Warsaw and during the death march from Warsaw to Dachau, and nineteen in Kaufering. He slaved away for such companies as Holzmann, Moll, and Messerschmitt. He burrowed deep into the ground, he laid track, he hauled stones, sacks of flour, bags of cement and crates of unknown contents; he leveled streets and squares, he secured the bolts of the pipe linkage for the preliminary drillings; he tore down walls, he cleaned the bricks for reuse, he climbed up chimneys, he worked with explosives, he planted an acre of potatoes, he dug out mass graves, he gathered the bodies. At the very beginning he felled trees. When he was twenty, he found himself standing in a line in front of an American officer in Bad Tölz who was asking everyone: what is your name, where are you going. His only friend, a Frenchman by the name of André Lubka, answered: to France.

He actually did have one other friend, the Belgian Henri, whom Liebermann, the Kapo in Birkenau, wanted to kill. Every Sunday a Croatian in the SS tried to set two prisoners against one another. But first he pulled down their pants, to see what they had. Liebermann was the strongest of all the inmates. He charged at the Belgian because he knew, I will make short order of this guy. But he hadn't counted on Willi. Later on, in Warsaw, Henri reciprocated by tossing Willi some clothes — a striped pair of pants and a paper-thin shirt — when he jumped naked out of the window of the sickbay as the SS soldiers were about to mow down the prisoners.

Liebermann was lucky. After the liberation they nearly beat him to death. Some time later he was tried in France and sentenced to ten years in prison.

So Willi also said: to France, and he too was issued a permit. He would have gone to France in any case, since he had promised something.

He had a god all his own. That was certainly one advantage. So also was the fact that he had learned at an early age to do without some things. He had never had the experience of sleeping on white sheets. It was especially an advantage that he had never forgotten what it was like to be hungry, and that he had never lost his hatred of his tormentors. Whoever hates, won't give up. His sixth sense, which prevented him from making rash decisions, also proved useful. In Buchenwald, for example, he was the only one in his unit who never ate the mushrooms in the forest. He witnessed the white foam oozing from the mouths of the other inmates, their wide-opened eyes.

To Vienna? Why? To whom? There was no longer anyone there waiting for him. Except for Pepi Nowotny, if he had survived the war. But he only thought of Pepi years later.

And his presence of mind. One day in Kaufering he was going to the latrine when a bored SS officer leaned out of a window to summon Willi toward him. Which detail? Reporting, sir: garden duty. Where are you from? From Innsbruck, sir.. What did your father do? He was a blacksmith. Beat it! Afterwards he heard it said that that was Doctor Mengele. Had Willi answered: Vienna, tailor. So a Jew. He would probably not be alive today.

But he also did not stand for any nonsense. In Warsaw he was once knocked off the board leading to the latrine by a Greek prisoner, a dockworker from Salonika. All of the prisoners were lined up like chickens sitting on a perch. Willi got back up on his feet, jumped on the Greek and threw him into the filth. He knew that if I did not gain respect for myself then I'd be a goner.

In France he made the acquaintance of a woman, and together they immigrated to Chile. Elena was six years old at the time.

They disembarked with a hundred dollars in their pocket.

An SS man met them at the ramp in Birkenau. He had nervous thumbs: left, right, left, left, right. Left was gas. Willi was strong, so for him the thumb pointed right. He had to get fully naked and was then herded into the barracks with the others who had survived the selection process; ice-cold water was sprayed from the ceiling. He was forced to stand still for two days in the frosty winter of 1942; those who survived scurried back and forth loaded down with stones. Each was given a quarter liter of heavily-salted coffee substitute to drink. They thirsted. But the fountains they passed, adorned with flowers, were marked with warnings: "Attention. Do not drink. Poison." Those who nevertheless bent down to drink from the fountains died.

He never considered having the tattoo removed. Why? It is proof that he still is alive. The six-digit number is quite legible. He kept his arm steady. All the others moved.

In the evening a piece of bread and a dab of jam. The bread was rock hard, and the men fought for their share. He was still quite strong; he wouldn't be defeated. He beat the others. *That is the truth.*

The first thing that struck him was how soccer-crazy the Chileans were. On the day they arrived in Valparaíso, a Sunday, the streets were empty. Willi looked through the open windows; he saw men, teenagers, women and lovers sitting in front of the radio biting their nails or clenching their fists. A frenetic voice gave commentary on the game between the Santiago Wanderers and the Audax Italiano. There was enormous passion for soccer, but nothing to satisfy this enthusiasm. Table soccer was virtually unknown. So together with an unsuccessful poet, who had inherited a workshop, Willi began to build soccer tables. Two years later they had a thousand tables in taverns all around the country, from Antofagasta in the north down to Punta Arenas. Not a bad beginning.

"Canada," for example, was a good unit. They could always manage to get hold of something. One day, a transport arrived from Theresienstadt. When they opened the car doors, they saw the freight lying in unslaked lime. Small, burned children.

He never wanted to speak about it. But today is an exception. What happened, happened. Anyway, he is not an isolated case. There were millions of others. Most of them perished. How would his commentary change anything?

Wasserstein was supposedly a friend of his father. The two of them played cards together in the tavern in Ferdinandstraße. In Birkenau, he was the oldest in the barrack and never missed an opportunity to torture Willi. For example, he always made Willi serve the soup. The container was filled to the brim with steaming hot water in which a couple of potatoes floated. With each step across the uneven stone floor, some of the soup spilled over and scorched Willi's hands and feet. In vain, he begged Wasserstein to relieve him, at least for one day. Wasserstein was later not to survive the transport from Auschwitz to Warsaw.

In Santiago, he managed, either subsequently or simultaneously, a hotel, several restaurants, a gas station, a garage, a car dealership, a laundry and a factory that produced plastic piping. At one time, he had a hundred and fifty employees. He was able to afford a small house, which he rented, then a second, which he also rented, a summer home in Algarrobo, ditto, and a third house, in which he lives today, with Elena.

For a quarter of a century he did not know what vacation was.

Once he risked it. No one noticed. It worked again the next day. Finally it became a habit to eat twice at mealtime. He quickly downed the first portion, ran outside, and got in line again – until one day someone grabbed him by the collar, hauled him into the block, forced him head first into the chimney and pulled down his pants. They beat his behind bloody with an electric cord. And off to the penal commando.

Willi is very grateful to the Chileans, that they allowed him into their country without asking a lot of questions, that they took him and his family in, that they let him work there. By and large, he got along well with the Chileans. He kept his distance from the German colony to the extent that that was possible from a business perspective.

He stood in shit up to his chest. With a piece of wood, a kind of paddle, he had to stir up the excrement, to keep it watery, so that the pump could suck it up. That was his work, day in and day out. In the evening he waded out of the pool and dragged himself to his wooden hovel. His cellmates could not bear his stench. Only at night did Lieutenant Colonel Schillinger take his eyes off him. The next morning he was always there, at a safe distance, to make sure that Willi was still alive. After six weeks, he bellowed, you, Jewish bastard, you're not dead yet, back to the cellblock.

The better quarters never interested him. He didn't like Providencia, Las Condes even less, Vitacura not at all. Nuñoa, hardworking simple people, was much better.

Then, after the transfer to the main camp in Auschwitz, the waiting in the shower barracks. Not a drop of water. What might that mean? Men crammed tightly together, with raised heads. The trembling of the pupils. Lips that silently counted the seconds. The tears afterward, the sobbing, when water finally came out of the showerheads.

Elena's brother was born in Chile in 1953. That was a great surprise. Willi hadn't figured on that.

Ten years difference in age, just as between him and his own brother. They, however, have an intimate relationship, even today. Hardly a day passes that they don't see each other.

One morning he marched to the workplace. He suddenly found himself at the head of his detail, carrying a shovel; a little further on, there was another work detail, likewise marching. All women. All at once he heard a woman cry: Willi, Willi! The woman took two steps out of formation toward him, and the dogs attacked her, dragged her to the ground. An SS man runs to her, says something, pulls out his pistol, shoots her.

He knew right away, that's my mother, but he felt nothing.

Even today he cannot explain it. That he felt nothing. Why he didn't run to her. The SS would have shot him down too, but at least he would have died with his mother.

He simply kept on marching. He did hear another woman call, Willi, be strong! and he felt nothing. He thinks about this often. Every night. He has to take Lexatin every night. Occasionally he tried to stop taking the drug. Then it is just terrible. Then he hears his mother screaming. Every night. Without fail. *Always, always, always.*

His sister was also there in Auschwitz, in the women's commando. Yes, it was she who called: be strong, Willi! No, she did not survive either.

He never beat around the bush in front of the children. His wife was the same. He wanted them to understand the difference between democracy and dictatorship. And they never forgot his lesson. But he did all that he could to keep them out of politics when they were young, when so many young people considered the revolution possible and necessary.

Everywhere rubble, billowing smoke, glowing ambers of unextinguished fires. A few days after the revolt, the ghetto looked like it had been bombed. The command was to level the Warsaw ghetto. They had to carry off the forty or fifty-meter chimneys brick by brick. Soon he no longer looked up when someone near him fell to the ground. Later on he was assigned to a demolition squad; he drilled holes into the walls, stuck the dynamite cartridges in, and sealed the holes with dirt. The fuse ran to the German explosive experts, who blew forcefully in their horns. Once he was standing high up in the ruins of a house, in a doorframe, and was not able to get away. The house collapsed. Only one wall remained standing, a single door on the second floor, and in the door Willi.

In 1979 Allende was elected. Willi was convinced that things would take a turn for the worse. He knew the middle class, he knew the mood of the army, he already smelled the blood. But Elena and her brother were enthusiastic. They wanted to participate in the peaceful march to Socialism. In order to prevent them, he said, even if nothing were to happen to them, he himself would certainly be targeted. He could stand the torture. He could put up with having to dig his own grave. He would bear being burned alive. He would endure everything, except the knowledge that his children might suffer. So they stayed away. But they stood on the right side.

At Yom Kippur there was bread. Pious Jews from his transport, twenty men perhaps, refused to eat. The shouts of a Kapo drew the attention of an SS man. With pistol drawn, he demanded that they bite, chew, swallow. The Jews still refused. Then, in a deliberate manner, he shot them in the head, one by one.

He, too, of course. Absolutely. He makes no secret of it. Who knows whether he would not have gone along if it had not been for his wife.

The family, his wife were his support. Otherwise, of course he would have.

The worst were the children of the SS. Kids, no bigger

than the rifle they carried. They always had their finger on the trigger.

But the unpredictability, the lack of logic. Arbitrary and routine murder. But when it rained, they did not have to head out to work.

In September 1973 there was the military putsch, something that he had foreseen. But he did not get involved. He behaved as if the whole thing were of no consequence to him. He continued to pay his taxes on time, he paid his bills, and he adhered to all deadlines. He did whatever it took not to be noticed. He hoped he would simply be overlooked.

Once he was squatting in a basement in Warsaw. There was an explosion and the shock wave sent a whole sack of bread flying toward him, warm, freshly baked bread. Another time, also in Warsaw and likewise in a cellar, he found a small box filled with jewelry. One of the Poles, who had put up the wall around the former ghetto, gave him an onion and a tiny piece of bread for it. And a third time, still again in Warsaw, he was infected with typhus. A tall Greek fellow was lying with him on the plank bed; he had been dead for days, but Willi did not report it so that he could get the man's rations. A fourth time, when he arrived at Dachau, they rushed the bread depot. The SS fired into the crowd. Despite the shots, his friend Lubka was able to steal some bread, which he then shared with Willi.

For example he had an apartment on the first floor. And one night, after the coup, he heard brakes screeching and doors slamming, even some muffled cries. He peeked out of the window, saw a car with three or four men stopped outside; they jerked a very young man from the trunk, threw him beneath the window and then trampled him to death with their boots.

Hunger is the motivation for everything. Injustice, that is where it all begins. In Chile, in Vienna, and elsewhere. At the moment he is thinking of Argentina. The property owners, they are the bandits, they have robbed the country. You have to imagine: this is a country that could feed a third of humanity. There is plenty of cattle, grain, oil, and gold. There is something to harvest every season. And yet five out of ten Argentinians go hungry. Something is just not right.

In Kaufering a large potato slipped out of his shirtsleeve. They rammed the potato into his mouth; then they forced him into the strip between the two electrified fences. There he had to stand at attention – without moving. In front of him a watchtower, the sentries laughed and teased him. He held out for two days and two nights. On the third day he was allowed to go back to the block; he spit the potato out. With his mouth locked wide open, he just stood there; his jaw stiff, as if rusted in place.

Earlier in Warsaw, he had taken a potato from the kitchen and hid it in his pants. There too he was caught; as punishment he was transferred to a detail on the Weichsel where he had to unload ships that carried war spoils from Russia. Sacks with food supplies were his salvation. Here, all he had to do was stick the food in his mouth.

Given the current economic crisis many of his tenants are unable to pay their rent. What is he supposed to do; he cannot simply put them out on the street.

In the evening they were returned to the camp in a truck. They squatted on the flatbed, under the tarp, a sentry armed with a machine gun on the running board. One day they found themselves under attack by Soviet planes. A bomb exploded just in front of the truck. It ripped off the motor hood, hurled the cab of the truck through the air, and tore the SS man to pieces. Only Willi and two other prisoners were unhurt. They ran down the street, knocked on some doors, begged for entry. Finally he was free. No one opened. Freedom consisted of his being allowed to walk back to the camp.

He was always a leftist. He is a leftist today. For his whole life he shared the leftist perspective. Even as a child. He grew up as a leftist. He can still remember the May Day festivities in Vienna, the demonstrations in the Prater, and the coaches with the red and white floral arrangements. That is simply splendid, one cannot forget that. Perhaps today he is even more a leftist than he was before. Although he has made something of his life and although he can get along now without having to rely on the left, he has remained a leftist. A leftist businessman, why not.

When a new camp was built in Warsaw next to the provisional one, a camp with real wooden barracks, the prisoners were separated. Sixty men, including Willi, were to remain behind. But his Kapo, who wore a green patch, whispered to him, stand over here next to me. Willi joined his ranks, and marched over to the new camp. At roll call there was one prisoner too many. After the third count off, the SS men sent someone else, not Willi, back to the camp. Later Willi learned that the sixty prisoners had to burn the old camp down. Then they were shot.

His wife died on 25 March 1979, a Sunday, almost thirty years to the day after their arrival. Quite suddenly, of a stroke. He had brought her breakfast in bed and then left because he had the car dealership at the time and was supposed to show a customer a new model. He would be back by midday. Then we'll have siesta together, promise me, she said. He gave her a kiss and promised her. That was ten-thirty. At twelve-thirty he came home, the apartment door was open but chained. He called and knocked, but she did not come. He tried to break the chain, but couldn't, so he kicked the door in. He ran to the kitchen, saw the roast in the oven and the dessert on the serving table, ran into the bedroom, the bed was made, ran into the bathroom, the faucet dripped, then he opened the door to the toilet. There she lay on the floor.

This was in the summer of 1944, during the revolt by the Polish underground army, when Willi was in sickbay with double pneumonia. The SS men stormed the infirmary and shot all those who were sick. All except him; naked, he had jumped out of the first floor as the Belgian Henri tossed him some clothes. Since communications to Berlin were disrupted, the SS men did not know what to do. At first they commanded the prisoners to dig a mass grave. Then they decided to escape to the West. They hitched the prisoners to the front of the horse carts on which they stored their luggage – suitcases, bags, household goods. Before he jumped up onto the driver's bench, a Croatian tied a rope around Willi's neck. At some point Willi was able to loosen the knot and to disappear into the column. During this march from Warsaw to Dachau, he escaped. Once, he took a deep breath, and there was no longer a sharp pain in his lung.

Everything recalled her presence. Every room and all the appliances. The clock on the wall, the clothes in the closet, the cake tin, the key rack, the sugar bowl. The soap, cotton balls, the bottles, her very scent, which did not let go of him, which he sought, which overwhelmed him. The grim determination, with which he wanted to continue living with his dead wife, was against all reason. He had to do something. He rented a room in a pension – Elena was married then, her husband was still alive – and sought a buyer for his house. Because of his impatience he sold it far below its market value.

In Dachau he became friends with three men, German prisoners with shorn heads, who had large placards hanging from their necks: "I am a Freemason pig!" The men opened his eyes, talked to him about things that he had never comprehended. He began to understand. He had lived with a terrible hatred, and they showed him that there is something else in life. One day all three were hanged. He was quite shaken by their deaths.

But not just the house – the Cerro Santa Lucía, the Río Mapocho, the Quinta Normal, the whole city reminded him of his wife. Every café, every bakery, every face on the street, all the shoes of the passers-by, the stands at the Ferjas Persas, the valley of the Río Maipo, the voices on television and the smog over Santiago.

In Kaufering he was assigned to the death commando. They dug a mass grave and gathered the corpses. In the summer they stank, in the winter they were frozen stiff, with twisted limbs. He had to break their arms and legs, and with the help of a hammer he shattered their jaws in order to recover the gold fillings. In broad daylight they pulled the cart through the village. They sang as they pulled. The Dutch Kapo sat enthroned on the top of the mountain of bodies as he cursed and whipped them. When he once went too far, they yanked the shaft sharply to the side. The cart overturned, and the Kapo was buried alive beneath the dead bodies. He broke a leg, cursed and whined; someone pulled off his boot, Willi pissed in it.

He always makes the same mistake. When something happens, he thinks if you walk away . . . but that doesn't help. He knows it. It haunts you wherever you go. The problem has to be solved where it first appears.

Singing with all their might. Songs from the wine taverns, hits, counting verses, whatever occurred to them at the moment. "I had two spunky horses." "I know a hotel in the fourth district." "On the hill sits a Croate." "Up on the hill sits a cow, who opens her ass and closes it now." Singing anything, just singing, out of defiance.

Suddenly he's gone. Further south, to Concepción. If he made a mistake, . . . but it worked out all right.

Of course, contact between the men's camp and the women's camp was forbidden. But an underground tunnel connected the two camps, and one night he crawled through the pipe. At the fence he talked to two sisters from Hungary, one named Hajna Rothstein. Hajna was an attractive blonde girl, but it would never have occurred to him to kiss her or even to touch her. Everything in him was dead. But the need for tenderness was there. He brought her something to eat, as well as a pair of red boots that he had taken off the feet of a dead woman. A few days later a transport departed, to Bergen-Belsen. *Finished.* He never saw the Rothstein sisters again.

Elena suffered a great deal when her mother died. She was very attached to her. Now she takes care of him, just as her mother had done. Besides, he's not a young man anymore, something really could happen to him. Perhaps that stems from her childhood: the constant fear that she has.

An SS man asked, do any of you have experience in gardening. Willi stepped forward. He understood nothing of the sort. But in such a situation everyone knows something.

They are so different, Elena and her brother. But Willi never really dwelled on the difference. Neither did his wife. Or did he? It may be that he showed some preference for Elena. In any case, he worried more about her.

Then came the command to plant potatoes. Willi said, I can't do that alone, I need some additional people. OK, we will give you a women's detail. There were ten, twelve, or perhaps fifteen women. Some carried wooden baskets across the soil, one basket on each side, others dug holes with their hoes. Willi's job was to stick a potato in each hole. A super detail, if it weren't for –

Today it is just the opposite. Today his son worries him more. He used to be just as devoted as Elena. Now he goes his own way, comes home late, leaves early, and doesn't say much. Willi doesn't know what has got into him.

Yes, he does. A young widow has turned his head. A woman from a clan of plantation owners from the region around Loncoche, who considered Allende the devil himself and who didn't wash themselves for a month if one of the generals had shaken their hand. He feels ashamed when he is with her, for his father. Because he has hands like shovels. Hopefully not because he has an arm with a number on it.

That was during the evacuation march through Bavaria, as they moved through the foothills of the Alps. It was the end of April or the beginning of May '45, and there was still snow on the ground. The men collapsed of exhaustion; they lay motionless on the ground or crawled on all fours before they were shot by the guards. Willi looked neither left nor right. He moved forward at a steady pace, like a robot. He had a belt tied around his waist, which he had used to drag the dead bodies. Little Fritz, a dwarf from Berlin who had been housed in the experimental block in Auschwitz, now held on tightly to the belt. Then there was another prisoner, a cattle dealer by profession, but Willi drove him off because he had once betrayed him. Next to him staggered his friend Lubka, who moaned, it is over, finished, I can't go on. As Lubka leaned on him, Willi took him by the arm. The dwarf behind him, the friend on the right. But on the second or third day Lubka was clearly finished. Carried him on his back. Along came an SS man, put his revolver to Willi and shouted: Drop him! Bent over with his load and with the dwarf Fritz at his belt, Willi said –

Willi could not have cared less. He would not have abandoned his friend.

Stick it up your ass!

The SS man stared at him, incredulous, as if he couldn't believe what he had just heard. Then he made a dismissive motion with his hand, laughed, and turned away.

This was in Bad Tölz. In the afternoon. There was a gravel pit in the middle of the woods. Up at the edge of the pit the SS men had positioned their machine guns. They commanded the prisoners to lie flat on the ground. Willi assumed that they would be shot in the pit. He pulled a dead body over himself as a protective shield; Lubka followed suit. But nothing happened. Night fell. He wanted to sleep, but his eyes would not close. The following morning the sky was cloudless. The sun was shining, the birds were chirping. He and Lubka crawled carefully out from under the corpses; they slid onto their knees, and stood up. No reaction from the top of the pit. They climbed up the slope, saw the machine guns, no trace of the guards.

There was an infirmary for the SS in the city where sick and injured men were lying on wonderfully white sheets.

They threw the men out of the beds. They dragged them through the hallways and hurled them out the windows.

One of them bit through the throat of an SS man. They hunted down the Kapos who had tortured them.

To tell the truth, I am not proud of what I did then.

But earlier in Kaufering, one day in the garden, a woman from his detail –

He never spoke about it. Never. *Never, never, never,* and he will never speak about it again.

A French woman. Yes, a Jew.

How can he know that? He never asked her age. Perhaps in her early thirties.

She stumbled or slipped, in any case she fell on a rock.

Her knee-cap was shattered. That was her death sentence. She knew it. The SS killed her. But before she would die, she had to tell him something, he had to promise her something, and he kept his promise. There on the field. There was no other opportunity.

That she has a child, and the child's name is Hélène and she is hidden in a cloister in France, at so and so, and he should take care of the child if he is fortunate enough to live through the ordeal.

Now you know.

He had time to ask her: Are there relatives, her sister or her mother, anyone in the family? No. It is true that at that point he stopped asking. *That is the truth.* Perhaps there would have been someone else.

If for example he had known of the father, he lives here, or this is where an aunt lives —

If the child's father had still been alive, she would have said so. There was enough time for that.

So, off he went to France. He had to keep his word. The promise.

In Lille he was admitted to a clinic, along with many other concentration camp survivors. But on the second or third day after his arrival, or perhaps a week later —

I am her father, he said. The nuns did not ask many questions. They were happy when someone relieved them of their responsibility. Besides, Elena was an only child. Surely there were hundreds of such children. Or women, who thought that their husband was dead and then remarried and had children, and when the husband returned, he understood that his wife had a new family or vice versa; the husband never remarried.

He said, listen, my wife was also in a concentration camp, she is not back yet, but I know she is alive. Then it is better that we wait. Yes, I will wait for her, and when she is here, we'll take the child with us. All in due time, one of them said, perhaps it was the Mother Superior. No, he said, let's take care of the financial part right away. That is easier for me.

Selfishness – ? It's possible. Right at the beginning, the first time he laid eyes on Elena. She was so pitiful. He felt so sorry for her. She put her little hand in his. He took her into his heart right away. Also because he believed that he would never be able to have children.

Now he needed a wife. It was fortunate that young people from the city visited the survivors in the sanatorium, that they engaged in conversation with them, sat on the bench in the institution's park, brought them gifts, saw them as people. There was a young woman among them whom he liked. She liked him too. Her name was Thérèse.

She was two years older than he. He didn't play games with her. The child must have a mother. She said, if that is what you wish, then I am in agreement. No, he answered, you must want it for yourself. Yes, she said, that is what I want.

Her father died shortly after the war. He had worked in the resistance. He had just arrived home one day when the Gestapo came to arrest him. While his wife held the door closed, he jumped out the window. He was able to save himself, she was shot. Thérèse was an only child.

Willi had begun to work even before the wedding. In a textile factory. After work he attended evening school. He studied like a madman. He wanted to earn at least an elementary school diploma.

His wife had been through a great deal with him. He was psychically and physically broken. Each evening before he went to bed, he pushed the large dresser in front of the door. Under his pillow he hid bread. If someone had entered his room to take his bread – he would have shot him.

In sexual matters he also had problems. He simply couldn't do it. That was certainly one reason. But above all it was his promise, and that he felt so sorry for Elena, from the first moment that he saw her.

In contrast, life with her was a kind of healing.

He acquired the birth certificate in Marseilles. First, because he heard that it was easy to get counterfeit papers there. Second, Marseilles is at the other end of France. He had to assume that the forger might want to extort something from him. The greater the distance, the less the danger. So he traveled to Marseilles, followed the liaison to the forger's workshop, and wrote the required names and dates on the margin of a newspaper. The forger disappeared with the paper into a back room, and made him wait a half-hour. Then he brought him the documents. Good work. Willi paid the agreed upon amount, added another bill, left the basement shop, and took a roundabout way to the train station.

According to the birth certificate, he was hardly eighteen when she was born. So? How many people have a child at sixteen?

One day his brother appeared at the door.

Willi's brother had emigrated from Switzerland to England. When the war was over, he began to look for his relatives. From the Red Cross he found out that only Willi had survived. He went to Lille. He saw Elena, he asked who she was, Willi revealed his secret to him. His brother disapproved. He reproached him. He also objected to Willi's wife. Willi threw him out. He never saw him again. He said we're going to emigrate.

March 1949. First, because there was talk of a third world war in Europe. Willi had no interest in going through the whole thing again. Second, he did not want to be dependent on anyone. All he wanted was to create a life for himself and his family, and South America was better suited for that. The third and most decisive reason was that he wanted to erase all traces of his past. In France he lived in constant fear that the truth would come out one day. That Elena wasn't his daughter and that she would learn the truth. That's why he also had to alter his own life story. Not totally, but to some extent.

She did not ask many questions. Sometimes she wanted to hear it. He told her that he fled from Vienna right after the invasion of the Germans. Two years later the German army attacked France. He was in possession of good papers and passed himself off as an Alsatian. He was able to live undetected for quite a while. But how did the two of you actually meet, she asked. The first time I saw your mother was in the cinema. In the theater, after the showing, when the lights went back on. She sat two seats down from me; the seat between us was not taken. I didn't dare look at her. I only spoke to her afterwards. What kind of movie did you see? Her laughter, a comedy, I fell in love with her laugh. And then I was born, said Elena. No, not for some time. Someone revealed to me that the Germans were also after her, and so your mother and I fled to the south, secretly over the demarcation line. In early 1942 the Germans also occupied the south. A few months later Thérèse got pregnant. I was arrested shortly after that. Why did she go back then? She had to live off something, right? Her parents had remained in Lille. Then I was born. Then you were born. The Gestapo was already looking for your grandfather, and your grandmother had died. Your mother didn't know what to do, and so she had you hidden in the cloister. Just in time. Two days later she was arrested. She was in a concentration camp too? Yes. She never speaks about it. You shouldn't ask her about it. Why not? Because I said so.

He broke off contact with Europe. He never wrote letters. Nor did his wife. He does not know what became of his brother. He is certainly dead. It is of no interest to him. His friend Lubka is the only person he would like to see. And Pepi Nowotny, he could still be alive. Perhaps he will run into him on the street when he takes Elena and her brother to Vienna. Or maybe they would walk by without recognizing one another.

He wasn't afraid. But his wife was worried that he could get into trouble with the authorities over the forged documents. But that's over. There never were any problems. In Chile he even had a new birth certificate made for Elena, in Spanish; witnesses confirmed that he and his wife were the birth parents.

Sometimes he sits on the bench next to the grill and stares at his life as if at a chessboard. Sometimes he lies in bed and sees that half of his life is a lie. But the lie was worth it. On balance, what he did was indeed worthwhile. He doesn't have any regrets. He never did anything evil.

The joy that she brought him can never be repaid.

You will get to know her. You will see her. You will see that I haven't deceived you. Everything is fine. She manages the household, she goes out, she has fun, she has her own bank account, she doesn't need me, and in spite of that she is there for me.

Of course there are millions of people who know they are adopted, and they cope with it just fine. But he did not want that. He didn't want her to be burdened by her past. Her mother's horrific death; *that would have troubled her forever.* He wanted to give her a good life, a life without the truth: the mother was shot or beaten to death, or whatever they did to her.

He does not dare imagine how Elena would react.

For the children here in South America, who were stolen from their parents and raised in the military, it's different. They suffered. All of them suffered. Elena did not suffer.

Supposing that she were capable of harming herself.

Definitely. And if not, then the relationship between them would certainly be different. On her part, no longer love but gratitude. And that's not for him.

I don't want gratitude! Do you understand me, I want love.

(2003)

Afterword

Documenting the Forgotten: Realism, Fiction, and Morality

I

Born in Steyr in 1954, Erich Hackl is one of Austria's most significant contemporary writers. Known primarily for his well-received, book-length documentary narratives, the free-lance author has also edited books on third-world literature, compiled stories by German-speaking writers on the Spanish Civil War, and translated the poetry and novels of numerous Latin American writers into German. The many awards bestowed upon him testify to the importance of his work, e.g., the Solothurn Literature Prize (2002) for his *oeuvre*, the Lutheran Book Prize of the Association of German Lutheran Book Dealers (1991) for *Abschied von Sidonie* (*Farewell Sidonia*), the Bruno Kreisky Prize (1996) for *In fester Umarmung* (Dearly Embraced), and the Literary Prize of the City of Vienna (2002) for *Die Hochzeit von Auschwitz. Eine Begebenheit* (The Wedding in Auschwitz: An Event). While Hackl's works are regularly reviewed in the major German periodicals, he is, despite his noteworthy productivity and broad success, not particularly well known in the English-speaking world. This edition is intended to draw attention to his writings.

Hackl's essential achievement as a narrator lies in his willingness to chronicle authentic lives. In the tradition of Latin American testimonial literature (Miguel Barnet), he documents the individual lives of the powerless as they are stymied by political repression, social segregation, persecution, deprivation, and disenfranchisement. The minimally poetized reconstruction of individual histories (Kristina Maidt-Zinke speaks of the author's "poetic historiography")[1] becomes an expression of a social consciousness as well as a pedagogical tool. Through his characters, Hackl wants to offer his Austrian readers (and others as well) an alternative perspective on the impact that major socio-historical events have on individual lives. His simple, gentle yet occasionally angry prose can be understood as a means toward the establishment of a more just society, as the author himself observes: "I am interested in the conjunction of individual happiness and collective justice."[2] In his writing, he elaborates the egocentric behavior of those who side with the powerful as well as their desire to forget the past, thus rendering the possibility for a just and humane future more complicated. But Hackl's principal figures, despite their suffering, do not abandon their leftist, 'enlightened' reason (however out of fashion that may be) or their belief in a love that accords with human dignity. Their historical consciousness and their rejection of a sense of servility carry them in their quest for a moral community. Still, even as the longing for a community of like-minded individuals is strong, Hackl's heroes and heroines also communicate a sense of existential isolation. There remains in each of them a kind of social stigma, the result of their experience of exclusion, which distances them from the intolerant attitudes and practices of their social milieu and underscores their aloneness.

Given the unfamiliarity of the American reading public with Hackl's writings, it may be useful to review some of the author's major texts (which have been translated into English, Danish, Dutch, Hungarian, Italian and Spanish). One shies away from using the word 'novel' since the texts are frequently documentary in nature, that is, they incorporate authentic historical documents. Moreover, Hackl guides his reader by offering an indication of the genre in the title or subtitle of his texts, such as story, report, event, endless story, reflections, sketch or recollection, and novel. By his own admission, Hackl understands himself as part narrator and part historian. His works are the result of thorough research mixed sparingly with poetic embellishment in a carefully crafted, sober yet eminently readable language. For Hackl's aim is to remain as faithful to the linguistic reality and personal ethos of his everyday characters as possible. Hackl's first narrative *Auroras Anlaß* (1987), translated as *Aurora's Motive*,[3] drew critical attention not only for its bold opening sentence – "One day Aurora Rodríguez was compelled to kill her daughter," but also for the aesthetic stance it announced, i.e., here is a historical account of Aurora Rodríguez, whose hopes for more justice for women in pre-Franco Spain could have been realized by her daughter Hildegart. The author's second substantial publication, *Abschied von Sidonie*, translated as *Farewell Sidonia*,[4] is another meticulously researched story. It deals with a gypsy girl, Sidonie, who is adopted as an infant by a Social-Democratic couple in Steyr in 1934 and then ultimately betrayed by the self-protective Austrian population who sends her to her death in Auschwitz in 1943. *Sara und Simón. Eine endlose Geschichte* (Sara and Simón. An Endless Story), published in 1997, further delineates Hackl's aesthetic of documentation and his representation of the disenfranchised as the author unravels the tale of the Uruguayan Sara Méndez who, because of her political activism against the Uruguayan dictatorship in the 1970s, is robbed of her twenty-day-old child Simón and then imprisoned and tortured. Upon her release, she endures the collusive behavior of her countrymen in an ultimately successful quest to find her child. 1999 saw the publication of *Entwurf einer Liebe auf den ersten Blick* (*Love at First Sight: A Recollection*) in which Hackl, again drawing on historical events and documents, relates the story of the love between Karl Sequens, an Austrian who fought with the International Brigade in the Spanish Civil War, and Herminia Roudière Perpiñá, a strong and engaged Spanish woman. Their fate and the subsequent life of their daughter provide the chronological frame and the ethos of the work. In 2000 Hackl translated the Guatemalan Rodrigo Rey Rosa's *El cojo bueno* (which has been rendered into English as *Good Cripple*) as *Die verlorene Rache*, and in 2001 he translated Rosa's *Que me maten si* . . . (1997) as *Die Henker des Frieden*s (The Executioners of Peace), both of which deal with the Civil War in Guatemala. Rosa's pristine prose and political-moral orientation resemble Hackl's own social-aesthetic stance. Hackl's next significant publication, the multi-voiced *Die Hochzeit von Auschwitz. Eine Begebenheit* (2002) (The Wedding in Auschwitz: An Event), offers a loosely connected array of first-person perspectives by those familiar with the events surrounding the extraordinary wedding that took place in Auschwitz in March 1944 between the Spaniard Maria Ferrer and the Austrian Rudi Friemel. Lacking an omniscient narrator, the lucid, insistent language of the text suggests that the wedding be seen as a hopeful act of resistance to the Nazi contempt for humanity. Hackl's most recent work, *Anprobieren eines Vaters. Geschichten und Erwägungen* (2004) (Trying On a Father: Stories and Reflections), is a collection of short pieces that includes "History of a Promise."

II

Love at First Sight: A Recollection is fairly typical of Hackl's writing in that it exudes the author's high regard for the ideals of Spanish republicanism and his deep affection for Spanish culture. (After studying German and Spanish in Salzburg and Málaga, Hackl lectured at the universities of Madrid and Vienna.) Moreover, the text, which the author characterizes as an outline or plan of a novel, is a carefully researched account of the lives of three individuals against a historical backdrop that includes the significant events of the First Republic of Austria, the Spanish Civil War, the Nazi terror, and the postwar years in Bavaria and Vienna. Through allusion, insinuation and sometimes direct expression, Hackl makes quite clear the repressive features of those periods as well as the egocentric behavior of those less principled than his heroes. As he surveys seven decades of history, Hackl portrays a simple love story in an even simpler language: the love between Karl Sequens and Herminia Roudière Perpiñá as it was told to him by the couple's daughter Rosa María. Besides her memory, the narrative also draws on a host of other sources that lend added credibility and perspective to the events: the comments of Karl's comrades, archival records, police registration forms, and Hans Landauer's memory. Hackl is also prepared to make suppositions about his characters, e.g., whether Karl and Herminia were able to see each other in the camp. And it is not unusual for the chronicler Hackl to insert himself as an engaged narrator more forcefully in the narrative, thus challenging the separation of fiction and history, e.g., when he notes "This is how I imagine their love." (5)

But it is finally the author's ability to offer vivid pictures of his characters that captures the reader's interest, imagination, and admiration. Their genuine diligence, conscientiousness and resilience resonate with the reader. (Hackl's description of the photos from the wedding and from the war front offers an encapsulated form of such portraiture.)

Indeed, the truths of Hackl's stories are to be found in the character and decisions of his real-life figures. Of his choice for non-fictional individuals, Hackl observed, "I don't think that fantasy offers more possibilities than reality. Reality is often more radical, more surprising and more unexpected than what I can portray."[5] This preference also imposes a greater moral obligation on Hackl as a writer for "my heroines and heroes exist outside of the story; what happens to them, happens in their real lives. I have to do justice to people, not just literary figures."[6] Hackl aims to give his individuals the dignity that they deserve as human beings, and he is particularly interested in avoiding the "mocking disdain of humanity" that he has observed in the late works of Thomas Bernhard and in Jörg Haider.[7] Avoiding the pathetic and the kitschy, Hackl celebrates a wholesome and human sentimentality.

Hackl presents us with a Karl, who stands tall, literally and figuratively, and is committed, through his opposition to fascism, to the cause of social justice. A typical Hackl figure, he affirms outwardly what he holds privately even when it entails his suffering. With a singular seriousness of purpose he acts on his convictions during the February uprising in Vienna and in the Spanish Civil War. He is a young man from the working class with few opportunities, but he becomes a capable leader, who values the well-being of his comrades and remains convinced of their educability as well as that of humanity. We recall how he insists that his daughter should learn whatever she wants. He remains optimistic and displays neither cynicism nor hypocrisy. Karl's faith in humanity and in social democracy is supported and perhaps guided by his admiration for nature's beauty. His faithfulness to his comrades and to the cause of the Spanish Republic is only exceeded by his fidelity to his wife. His love of Herminia, a love at first sight, blossoms as a result of shared values: education, trust, literature, and human kindness. His love is genuine, absent any self-interest. He loves Herminia as she is, not for what he wants her to be. And, despite some awkwardness, he is able to express this love rather clearly in his letters from the camps, which Hackl italicizes to allow us direct access to Karl's humanity. In the end, Karl perishes, but he abandons neither his love for Herminia and his daughter nor his dream of a life together with them in Vienna, representative perhaps of a larger belief in humanity.

Herminia is a strong, courageous woman, as are many of Hackl's heroines, e.g., Aurora Rodríguez, Josefa Breirather. Unmarried despite several offers, she stands somewhat apart from the Spanish women. Her medical training at the university and her earlier liberal education, as well as her conversations with her father, have nurtured her intelligence and independence, which in turn enable her to survive the war-time experiences, as her savvy allows her to elude the trap set by the SS man in the train. Herminia does not fear hard labor, as she works in the camps and on the farm, delivers newspapers, and knits gloves. Despite the racism and belittlement she experiences during the war and in postwar Europe, she retains her belief in the basic decency of humanity. Indeed, she affirms a larger sense of humanity: not nationalistic, but cosmopolitan. While Herminia recognizes that wealth does determine social and personal relations, she is unwilling to accept such a view as permanent and inalterable. Unequivocally, she values ethical conduct, not wealth, as she instantly assists the Frenchman who is caring for the concentration camp refugees. Despite her strength, however, she is also delicate: she maintains her outward composure but then cries in her pillow, and she feels saddened when she is told that she is not as handsome as Karl's former fiancée. But perhaps most striking is her utter devotion to Karl, which guides her every decision. Together for only a short time, Herminia never forsakes her love for him, as she never deserts her daughter.

The story itself results from Rosa María's promise to record Herminia's life story. Capable and reliable, Rosa María admires and emulates the values of her mother – education, steadfastness, fidelity, self-reliance, and justice. Rosa María's values are challenged not only by the terror of the Nazi regime but also by the racism and economic self-interest of postwar Bavaria and Vienna. Hopeful if realistic, she does not ingratiate herself with the powers that demean humanity. She sees through her aunt's conniving and harassment, as well as the hypocrisy of the hospital administrator and the priest at Herminia's funeral. Unforgettable are the laced candies she is served by her father's family in Vienna. Rosa María learns to stand up for herself against the forces of oppression, e.g., against her first husband. Tall like her father, she seems also to have acquired his serious nature, and she ultimately honors his promise to live in Vienna. Like her mother, she refuses to join a political party and she similarly puts herself in the service of humanity as a nurse.

The conclusion of *Love at First Sight: A Recollection*, which finds Rosa María falling in love with the noble-minded Spanish teacher Manfred, is not atypical of Hackl's writing. *Sidonie* closes with the hope that other gypsy children were treated more humanely, and in a final version of *Sara and Simón* Sara does find her lost son. The hopeful rounding out of the narrative may leave the author open to the criticism that he excessively ennobles the political left.[8] But the optimism is merely a prelude to the final subsequent affirmation of a higher value: in response to Isidor Lang's comment at the end of the novel that Herminia's love of her daughter has cost her much, Herminia responds, with a glance at her daughter, that it was indeed worth it. It is as if Hackl wants once again to underscore that the love and care that human beings exhibit toward one another is the true measure by which they are judged.

III

At the close of "History of a Promise," another account that elaborates the loving relationship between a parent and a child, Willi indicates in nearly the same language as Herminia that his lie about Hélène's true past "was worth it" because it protected his adopted daughter from the unnecessary suffering that he experienced himself and that he observed in South America. By keeping the truth from her, Willi has enabled Hélène to lead a rewarding life: *You will get to know her. You will see her. You will see that I haven't deceived you. Everything is fine.* Moreover, Willi's love of Hélène has given him a fundamental orientation in "the essential senselessness of historical developments."[9] Having been forced by social and political conditions to behave in ways that he has found unspeakably abhorrent, from the stealing as a young boy to the aggression in the camps to his response to the Kapos after their release, Willi can now relate the horrific events of his life with the knowledge that his love for Hélène and his wife has given it a more ethical shape. For the first time he speaks the truth about his life – *That is the truth* – and about his redemption through love: *I don't want gratitude! Do you understand me, I want love.* Desensitized (to the cries of his mother and to the charms of Hanja Rothstein) and necessarily self-reliant, Willi was nevertheless not maniacally self-absorbed, as his friendship with Lubka and his promise to assist Hélène in the convent indicate. Relationships make us human, and some bonds (one might say values) are possible even under the most extreme conditions. They are also apparent in the seemingly inevitable human impulse to engage in acts of resistance (singing, toppling the cart, defiant language) to the powers bent on callous destruction. These bonds are further evident when Willi has become a successful businessman. Recalling Herminia's father, Willi too is an enlightened, leftist entrepreneur; he does not take advantage of those who work for him nor of those who rent from him. His life has been fundamentally transformed by his love. It is a love that does not deny or eradicate the terror of his life, which remains unaccountably real, but it does affirm the possibility of moral conduct. Through his account, Willi, like Rosa María, expresses Hackl's own affirmation of the oppositional power of narrative: "The act of narration implies a belief, in spite of everything, in the capability of individuals to trust others. Narration is resistance – against forgetting, against the burying of experience, against the real or alleged destruction of trust, through which experience is communicated."[10]

The reader of "History of a Promise" will likely appreciate this complex, occasionally opaque text only after reading it a couple of times. For, although Hackl remains a chronicler and documentarist whose hero is again located in the uproar of history, he has chosen to abandon an auctorial narrator who might structure the story. Rather, he relies on the memory of the septuagenarian Willi to organize the events of the plot. In so doing, Hackl demonstrates that "My books are near literal reproductions of my conversations. With respect to the content, there is no invention other than some poetic embellishment. It is as if the characters' memories had gone directly into my story."[11] This strategy is risky, for the stages of Willi's life – his youth in Vienna, his early years in the camps, and his subsequent life in Chile – blend together in his mind. While the reader of "History of a Promise" is aided by the recurrence of some figures, e.g., Willi's brother, Lubka, Mr. Portemonnaie, Pepi Nowotny, the interwoven life stages refuse easy chronological sequencing. Reflecting the narrative position of *Die Hochzeit von Auschwitz*, in which past and present are linked without clear transition, Hackl may be responding to critics who have seen him as a traditional, inveterate realist.

The conversational tone of the text, which is strongly suggestive of an interview, reflects the author's intent to create the story out of Willi's memory, as when Willi states: "That was during the evacuation march..." But Willi's imprecise memory, or perhaps the colloquial absences of clear transitions, occasionally impedes our understanding, e.g., "'Canada,'for example, was a good unit. They could always manage to get hold of something. One day, a transport arrived from Theresienstadt. When they opened the car doors, they saw the freight lying in unslaked lime. Small, burned children." Clearly for Willi the sentences in this passage are related, but the reader wonders about the exact connection. Unanticipated conjunctions further underscore the informal, conversational thrust of the text and make demands on the reader: "If he made a mistake, but it worked out all right." Moreover, the reader is frequently thrown off balance, even if only momentarily, by the unclear pronoun references. One could assume, for example, that the "she" who stumbles in the story's first paragraph is also the woman in the second paragraph who is "slender, has long light-colored hair, wears a white blouse and blue linen pants with a braided leather belt." But that is not the case as the reader subsequently learns. Usually, the reference is more quickly clarified, as in "He too, of course. Absolutely. He makes no secret of it. Who knows whether he would not have gone along if it had not been for his wife." The failure to adhere to the common standards of punctuation, e.g., the omission of commas and question marks, further suggests the reminiscent quality of the narrative and causes the reader to wonder how to read a remark: "A leftist businessman, why not." Or "He never considered having the tattoo removed. Why?" Should the translator supply the question mark (as he did the explanatory note to "Krampus Day")? Hackl is inclined to use a period. Is he trying to capture Willi's tone? Perhaps the rules of grammar hold little meaning for the primary narrator, the aged Willi, as he may see both sides of an issue and have no need to express a question. Conversational language may also explain why Hackl shows little regard for parallelism, as if such formality were contextually inappropriate to the vagaries of historical reality: "When Hitler occupied Austria, they sat around the kitchen table in Pepi's house and cried, out of anger and because no one had come to their support." Likewise, the use of free indirect discourse, which the translator has consciously sought to maintain, is more illustrative of dialogic language and memory than of written prose: "Willi got back up on his feet, jumped on the Greek and threw him into the filth. He knew that if I did not gain respect for myself then I'd be a goner." In addition, there is generally little hypotaxis in the narrative. The lack of subordination places an additional burden on the reader; the portraitist Hackl prefers to state, not to explain, leaving the reader to account for the connections. The conflation of dialogues and other instances of ellipsis further compress the text and heighten the conversational tone: "Had Willi answered: Vienna, tailor. So a Jew. He would probably not be alive today." But when Hackl wants to affirm something unambiguously, he resorts to italics. Perhaps Willi pronounced them in a demonstrative manner in the interview. As Karl's letters were italicized to give the reader a greater sense of him as a character and to accentuate the importance of the comments, so Willi's brief italicized observations call attention to themselves: *To tell the truth, I am not proud of what I did then.* No doubt, he is not proud of what he did, but the conscientious reader understands Willi's conflict and its sympathetic portrayal.

In his reconstructive documentary literature Hackl reminds us pointedly that individual lives matter in the turbulent tide of history, and that there are bonds that connect us. Hackl's writing aims to provoke and direct reflection on what we decide to value in the real world, e.g., compassion, wealth, kindness, power, human rights. His writing illuminates social reality; at the end of *Sara und Simón* Hackl observes "At any rate, a life is more than a story."[12] Indeed, it is. While some segments of the American public might find Hackl's political convictions too far left (Ulrich Weinzierl speaks of Hackl's 'leftist humanism,')[13] the ethical commitment of his characters and their desire to achieve a more just and humane society (as they pursue their own happiness) should not be lost on any reader of Hackl's texts. Hackl's literature, with its wonderfully drawn real characters, offers encouragement that the battle for human rights should not be abandoned, and this is a particularly useful message in an age which finds those human rights under siege.

Edward T. Larkin
January, 2006

Selected Bibliography

Erich Hackl, "Geschichte erzählen? Anmerkungen zur Arbeit eines Chronisten." *Literatur und Kritik* (February 1995), 25 - 43.

Gabriele Eckart, "Latin American Dictatorship in Erich Hackl's Novel, *Sara und Simón*, and Miguel Asturias '*El Señor Presidente*." *The Comparatist* 25 (2001), 69 - 88.

Reimer, Robert C., "*Abschied von Sidonie*: A Farewell Twice-Visited: Erich Hackl's Novella and Karin Brandauer's Film." *After Postmodernism: Austrian Literature and Film in Transition.* Ed. Willy Riemer. Riverside, CA: Ariadne, 2000, 138 - 155.

Notes

[1] Kristina Maidt-Zinke speaks of the author's "poetische Historiographie" in *Frankfurter Allgemeine Zeitung*, April 30, 1999.

[2] In an interview in the *Solothurner Zeitung* of 12 December 2002, Hackl stated: "Das Thema, das mich interessiert, ist das Zueinanderfinden von individuellem Glück und Gerechtigkeit für alle."

[3] *Aurora's Motive*, translated by Edna McCown, New York: Knopf, 1989.

[4] *Farewell Sidonia*, translated by Edna McCown, Fromm International, 1991, Jonathan Cape, 1992. Hackl also wrote the screenplay for the Karin Brandauer film of 1990.

[5] "Ich glaube nicht, dass die Phantasie mehr Möglichkeiten bietet als die Realität. Die Wirklichkeit ist oft radikaler, überraschender und unverhoffter als das, was ich mir ausmalen kann." *Spiegel*, April 17, 1995.

[6] "Meine Heldinnen und Helden existieren auch außerhalb der Erzählung; was ihnen zustößt, stößt ihnen auch im wirklichen Leben zu. Ich muß Menschen gerecht werden, nicht literarischen Figuren." *Literatur und Kritik*, February 1995, 41.

[7] In an interview with *Wiener Anzeiger* (October 2002), Hackl speaks of the propensity of Thomas Bernhard and

Jörg Haider to indulge in the "Verächtlichmachen von Menschen."

[8] Eberhard Falcke suggests this in the *Süddeutsche Zeitung* (July 24, 1999): "Das respektvolle Mitgefühl des Autors für seine Figuren schlägt daher erzählerisch zuweilen um in den allzu schlicht intonierten Refrain vom linken Edelmut in einer bösen Welt." ("The respectful sympathy of the author for his figures occasionally results in the too neatly formulated refrain of leftist magnanimity in an evil world.")

[9] Hackl speaks of "die grundsätzliche Sinnlosigkeit geschichtlicher Abläufe" in his essay "Geschichte erzählen? Anmerkungen zur Arbeit eines Chronisten" in *Literatur und Kritik*, February 1995, 27.

[10] "Wer erzählt, glaubt trotz allem an die Fähigkeit des Menschen, anderen zu vertrauen. Erzählen sei Widerstand - gegen das Vergessen, das Verschütten von Erfahrung, die reale oder vorgebliche Zerstörung von Vertrauen, durch das sich Erfahrung mitteilt." *Literatur und Kritik*, February 1995, 41.

[11] Interview in the *Wiener Anzeiger* of October 2002. "Meine Bücher geben die Gespräche teilweise wortgetreu wieder. Inhaltlich gibt es keine Erfindung außer dem, was man Verdichtung nennt. Es ist, als wären die Erinnerungen durch meine Sprache gelaufen."

[12] "Ein Leben, immerhin, ist mehr als eine Geschichte." *Sara und Símon*, Zurich: Diogenes, 1998, 200.

[13] *Die Welt*, June 12, 2004 (4), 135.